The afternoon was already waning. The ancient countryside, scene to so many comings and goings, so much triumph and so much disaster, was laced with long black shadows. Looking down, Xanten reflected that though the human stock was native to this soil, and though his immediate ancestors had maintained their holdings for seven hundred years, Earth still seemed an alien world. The reason of course was by no means mysterious or rooted in paradox. After the Six Star War, Earth had lain fallow for three thousand years, unpopulated save for a handful of anguished wretches who somehow had survived the cataclysm and who had become semi-barbaric Nomads.

Then seven hundred years ago certain rich lords of Altair, motivated to some extent by political disaffection, but no less by caprice, had decided to return to Earth. Such was the origin of the nine great strongholds, the resident gentlefolk and the staffs of specialized andromorphs. Xanten flew over an area where an antiquarian had directed excavations, revealing a plaza flagged with white stone, a broken obelisk, a tumbled statue. The sight, by some trick of association, stimulated Xanten's mind to an astonishing vision, so simple and yet so grand that he looked around, in all directions, with new eyes. The vision was Earth, re-populated with men, the land cultivated, Nomads driven back into the wilderness.

At the moment the vision was far-fetched. . . .

THE
LAST CASTLE
JACK VANCE

SF
ace books
A Division of Charter Communications Inc.
A GROSSET & DUNLAP COMPANY
51 Madison Avenue
New York, New York 10010

THE LAST CASTLE

An ACE Book
by arrangement with the author

Published Simultaneously in Canada

2 4 6 8 0 9 7 5 3
Manufactured in the United States of America

CHAPTER ONE

1

Toward the end of a stormy summer afternoon, with the sun finally breaking out under ragged black rainclouds, Castle Janeil was overwhelmed and its population destroyed. Until almost the last moment factions among the castle clans contended as to how Destiny properly should be met. The gentlemen of most prestige and account elected to ignore the entire undignified circumstance and went about their normal pursuits, with neither more nor less punctilio than usual. A few cadets, desperate to the point of hysteria, took up weapons and prepared to resist the final assault. Still others, perhaps a quarter of the total population, waited passively, ready—almost happy—to expiate the sins of the human race. In the end, death came uniformly to all, and all extracted as much satisfaction from their dying as this essentially graceless process could afford. The proud sat turning the pages of their beautiful books, discussing the qualities of a century-old essence, or fondling a favorite Phane, and died without deigning to heed the fact. The hotheads raced up the muddy slope which, outraging all normal rationality, loomed above the parapets of Janeil. Most were buried under sliding rubble, but a few gained the ridge to gun, hack and stab, until they themselves were shot, crushed by the half-alive power-wagons, hacked or stabbed. The contrite waited in the classic posture of expiration—on their knees, heads bowed—and perished, so they believed, by a process in which the Meks were symbols and human sin the reality. In the end all were dead: gentlemen, ladies, Phanes in the pavilions; Peasants in the stables. Of all those who had inhabited Janeil, only the Birds survived, creatures awkward, gauche and raucous, oblivious to pride and faith, more concerned with the wholeness of their hides than the dignity of their castle. As the Meks swarmed down over the parapets, the Birds departed their cotes and, screaming strident insults, flapped east toward Hagedorn, now the last castle of Earth.

2

Four months before, the Meks had appeared

in the park before Janeil, fresh from the Sea Island massacre. Climbing to the turrets and balconies, sauntering the Sunset Promenade, from ramparts and parapets, the gentlemen and ladies of Janeil, some two thousand in all, looked down at the brown-gold warriors. Their mood was complex: amused indifference, flippant disdain, and a substratum of doubt and foreboding: all the product of three basic circumstances: their own exquisitely subtle civilization, the security provided by Janeil's walls, and the fact that they could conceive no recourse, no means for altering circumstances.

The Janeil Meks had long since departed to join the revolt; there only remained Phanes, Peasants and Birds from which to fashion what would have been the travesty of a punitive force. At the moment there seemed no need for such a force. Janeil was deemed impregnable. The walls, two hundred feet tall, were black rock-melt contained in the meshes of a silver-blue steel alloy. Solar cells provided energy for all the needs of the castle, and in the event of emergency, food could be synthesized from carbon dioxide and water vapor, as well as syrup for Phanes, Peasants and Birds. Such a need was not envisaged. Janeil was self-sufficient and secure, though inconveniences might arise when machinery broke down and there were no Meks to repair it. The situation then was disturbing but hardly desperate. During the day the gentlemen so inclined brought forth energy-guns and sport-rifles and killed as many Meks as the extreme range allowed.

After dark the Meks brought forward power-wagons and earth-movers, and began to raise a dike around Janeil. The folk of the castle watched without comprehension until the dike reached a height of fifty feet and dirt began to spill down against the walls. Then the dire purpose of the Meks became apparent, and insouciance gave way to dismal foreboding. All the gentlemen of Janeil were erudite in at least one realm of knowledge; certain were mathematical theoreticians, while others had made a profound study of the physical sciences. Some of these, with a detail of Peasants to perform the sheerly physical exertion, attempted to restore the energy-cannon to functioning condition. Unluckily, the cannon had not been maintained in good order. Various components were obviously corroded or damaged. Conceivably these components might have been replaced from the Mek shops on the second sub-level, but none of the group had any knowledge of the Mek nomenclature or warehousing system. Warrick Madency Arban* suggested that a workforce of Peasants search the warehouse, but in view of the limited mental capacity of the Peasants, nothing was done and the whole plan to restore the energy-cannon came to naught.

---

*Arban of the Madency family in the Warwick clan.

The gentlefolk of Janeil watched in fascination as the dirt piled higher and higher around them, in a circular mound like a crater. Summer neared its end, and on one stormy day dirt and rubble rose above the parapets, and began to spill over into the courts and piazzas: Janeil must soon be buried and all within suffocated. It was then that a group of impulsive young cadets, with more elán than dignity, took up weapons and charged up the slope. The Meks dumped dirt and stone upon them, but a handful gained the ridge where they fought in a kind of dreadful exaltation.

Fifteen minutes the fight raged and the earth became sodden with rain and blood. For one glorious moment the cadets swept the ridge clear and had not most of their fellows been lost under the rubble anything might have occurred. But the Meks regrouped and thrust forward. Ten men were left, then six, then four, then one, then none. The Meks marched down the slope, swarmed over the battlements, and with somber intensity killed all within. Janeil, for seven hundred years the abode of gallant gentlemen, and gracious ladies, had become a lifeless hulk.

3

The Mek, standing as if a specimen in a museum case, was a man-like creature native, in his original version, to a planet of Etamin. His tough rusty-bronze hide glistened metallically as if oiled or waxed; the spines thrusting back from scalp and neck shone like gold, and indeed were coated with a conductive copper-chrome film. His sense organs were gathered in clusters at the site of a man's ears; his visage—it was often a shock, walking the lower corridors, to come suddenly upon a Mek—was corrugated muscle, not dissimilar to the look of an uncovered human brain. His maw, a vertical irregular cleft at the base of this "face," was an obsolete organ by reason of the syrup sac which had been introduced under the skin of the shoulders; the digestive organs, originally used to extract nutrition from decayed swamp vegetation and coelenterates, had atrophied. The Mek typically wore no garment except possibly a work-apron or a tool-belt, and in the sunlight his rust-bronze skin made a handsome display. This was the Mek solitary, a creature intrinsically as effective as man —perhaps more by virtue of his superb brain which also functioned as a radio transceiver. Working in the mass, by the teeming thousands, he seemed less admirable, less competent: a hybrid of sub-man and cockroach.

Certain savants, notably Morninglight's D.R. Jardine and Salonson of Tuang, considered the Mek bland and phlegmatic, but the profound Claghorn of Castle Hagedorn asserted otherwise. The emotions of the Mek, said Claghorn, were different from human emotions, and only vaguely comprehensible to man. After diligent research Claghorn isolated over a dozen emotions.

In spite of such research, the Mek revolt came as an utter surprise, no less to Claghorn, D.R. Jardine and Salonson then to anyone else. Why? asked everyone. How could a group so long submissive have contrived so murderous a plot?

The most reasonable conjecture was also the simplest: the Mek resented servitude and hated the Earthmen who had removed him from his natural environment. Those who argued against this theory claimed that it projected human emotions and attitudes into a non-human organism, that the Mek had every reason to feel gratitude toward the gentlemen who had liberated him from the conditions of Etamin Nine. To this, the first group would inquire, "Who projects human attitudes now?" And the retort of their opponents was often: "Since no one knows for certain, one projection is no more absurd than another."

CHAPTER TWO

1

Castle Hagedorn occupied the crest of a black diorite crag overlooking a wide valley to the south. Larger, more majestic than Janeil, Hagedorn was protected by walls a mile in circumference, and three hundred feet tall. The parapets stood a full nine hundred feet above the valley, with towers, turrets and observation eyries raising even higher. Two sides of the crag, at east and west, dropped sheer to the valley. The north and south slopes, a trifle less steep, were terraced and planted with vines, artichokes, pears and pomegranates. An avenue rising from the valley circled the crag and passed through a portal into the central plaza. Opposite stood the great Rotunda, with at either side the tall Houses of the twenty-eight families.

The original castle, constructed immediately after the return of men to Earth, stood on the site now occupied by the plaza. The tenth Hagedorn, assembling an enormous force of

Peasants and Meks, had built the new walls, after which he demolished the old castle. The twenty-eight Houses dated from this time, five hundred years before.

Below the plaza were three service levels: the stables and garages at the bottom, next the Mek shops and Mek living quarters, then the various storerooms, warehouses and special shops: bakery, brewery, lapidary, arsenal, repository, and the like.

The current Hagedorn, twenty-sixth of the line, was a Claghorn of the Overwheles. His selection had occasioned general surprise, because O.C. Charle, as he had been before his elevation, was a gentleman of no remarkable presence. His elegance, flair, and erudition were only ordinary; he had never been notable for any significant originality of thought. His physical proportions were good; his face was square and bony, with a short straight nose, a benign brow, and narrow gray eyes. His expression, normally a trifle abstracted—his detractors used the word "vacant"—by a simple lowering of the eyelids, a downward twitch of the coarse blond eyebrows, at once became stubborn and surly, a fact of which O.C. Charle, or Hagedorn, was unaware.

The office, while exerting little or no formal authority, exerted a pervasive influence, and the style of the gentleman who was Hagedorn affected everyone. For this reason the selection of Hagedorn was a matter of no small importance, subject to hundreds of considerations, and it was

The clans of Hagedorn, their colors and associated families:

CLANS	COLORS	FAMILIES
Xanten	yellow; black piping	Haude, Quay, Idelsea, Esledune, Salonson, Roseth.
Beaudry	dark blue; white piping	Onwane, Zadig, Prine, Fer, Sesune.
Overwhele	gray, green; red rosettes	Claghorn, Abreu, Woss, Hinken, Zumbeld.
Aure	brown, black	Zadhause, Fotergil, Marune, Baudune, Godalming, Lesmanic.
Isseth	purple, dark red	Mazeth, Floy, Luder-Hepman, Uegus, Kerrithew, Bethune.

The first gentleman of the castle, elected for life, is known as "Hagedorn."

The clan chief, selected by the family elders, bears the name of his clan, thus: "Xanten," "Beaudry," "Overwhele," "Aure," "Iseth"—both clans and clan chiefs.

The family elder, selected by household heads, bears the name of his family. Thus "Idelsea," "Zadhause," "Bethune," and "Claghorn," are both families and family elders.

The remaining gentlemen and ladies bear first the clan, then the family, then the personal name. Thus: Aure Zadhause Ludwick, abbreviated to A.Z. Ludwick, and Beaudry Fer Dariane, abbreviated to B.F. Dariane.

the rare candidate who failed to have some old solecism or gaucherie discussed with embarrassing candor. While the candidate might never take overt umbrage, friendships were inevitably sundered, rancors augmented, reputations blasted. O.C. Charle's elevation represented a compromise between two factions among the Overwheles, to which clan the privilege of selection had fallen.

The gentlemen between whom O.C. Charle represented a compromise were both highly respected, but distinguished by basically different attitudes toward existence. The first was the talented Garr of the Zumbeld family. He exemplified the traditional virtues of Castle Hagedorn: he was a notable connoisseur of essences, and he dressed with absolute savoir, with never so much as a pleat nor a twist of the characteristic Overwhele rosette awry. He combined insouciance and flair with dignity; his repartee coruscated with brilliant allusions and turns of phrase; when aroused his wit was utterly mordant. He could quote every literary work of consequence; he performed expertly upon the nine-stringed lute, and was thus in constant demand at the Viewing of Antique Tabards. He was an antiquarian of unchallenged erudition and knew the locale of every major city of Old Earth, and could discourse for hours upon the history of the ancient times. His military expertise was unparalleled at Hagedorn, and challenged only by

D.K. Magdah of Castle Delora and perhaps Brusham of Tuang. Faults? Flaws? Few could be cited: over-punctilio which might be construed as waspishness; an intrepid pertinacity which could be considered ruthlessness. O.Z. Garr could never be dismissed as insipid or indecisive, and his personal courage was beyond dispute. Two years before, a stray band of Nomads had ventured into Lucerne Valley, slaughtering Peasants, stealing cattle, and going so far as to fire an arrow into the chest of an Isseth cadet. O.Z. Garr instantly assembled a punitive company of Meks, loaded them aboard a dozen power-wagons, and set forth in pursuit of the Nomads, finally overtaking them near Drene River, by the ruins of Worster Cathedral. The Nomads were unexpectedly strong, unexpectedly crafty, and were not content to turn tail and flee. During the fighting, O.Z. Garr displayed the most exemplary demeanor, directing the attack from the seat of his power-wagon, a pair of Meks standing by with shields to ward away arrows. The conflict ended in a rout of the Nomads; they left twenty-seven lean black-cloaked corpses strewn on the field, while only twenty Meks lost their lives.

O.Z. Garr's opponent in the election was Claghorn, elder of the Claghorn family. As with O.Z. Garr, the exquisite discriminations of Hagedorn society came to Claghorn as easily as swimming to a fish. He was no less erudite than

O.Z. Garr, though hardly so versatile, his principal field of study being the Meks, their physiology, linguistic modes, and social patterns. Claghorn's conversation was more profound, but less entertaining and not so trenchant as that of O.Z. Garr; he seldom employed the extravagant tropes and allusions which characterized Garr's discussions, preferring a style of speech which was unadorned. Claghorn kept no Phanes; O.Z. Garr's four matched Gossamer Dainties were marvels of delight, and at the viewing of Antique Tabards Garr's presentations were seldom outshone. The important contrast between the two men lay in their philosophic outlook. O.Z. Garr, a traditionalist, a fervent exemplar of his society, subscribed to its tenets without reservation. He was beset by neither doubt nor guilt; he felt no desire to alter the conditions which afforded more than two thousand gentlemen and ladies lives of great richness. Claghorn, while by no means an Expiationist, was known to feel dissatisfaction with the general tenor of life at Castle Hagedorn, and argued so plausibly that many folk refused to listen to him, on the grounds that they became uncomfortable. But an indefinable malaise ran deep, and Claghorn had many influential supporters.

When the time came for ballots to be cast, neither O.Z. Garr nor Claghorn could muster sufficient support. The office finally was conferred upon a gentleman who never in his most optimistic reckonings had expected it: a gentleman of decorum and dignity but no great depth; without flippancy, but likewise without vivacity; affable but disinclined to force an issue to a disagreeable conclusion: O.C. Charle, the new Hagedorn.

Six months later, during the dark hours before dawn, the Hagedorn Meks evacuated their quarters and departed, taking with them power-wagons, tools, weapons and electrical equipment. The act had clearly been long in the planning, for simultaneously the Meks at each of the eight other castles made a similar departure.

The initial reaction at Castle Hagedorn, as elsewhere, was incredulity, then shocked anger, then—when the implications of the act were pondered—a sense of foreboding and calamity.

The new Hagedorn, the clan chiefs, and certain other notables appointed by Hagedorn met in the formal council chamber to consider the matter. They sat around a great table covered with red velvet: Hagedorn at the head; Xanten and Isseth at his left; Overwhele, Aure and Beaudry at his right; then the others, including O.Z. Garr, I.K. Linus, A.G. Bernal, a mathematical theoretician of great ability, and B.F. Wyas, an equally sagacious antiquarian who had identified the sites of many ancient cities: Palmyra, Lubeck, Eridu, Zanesville, Burton-on-Trent, and Massilia among others. Certain family elders filled out the council: Marune and Baudune of Aure; Quay, Roseth and Idelsea of Xanten; Uegus of Isseth, Claghorn of Overwhele.

All sat silent for a period of ten minutes, arranging their minds and performing the silent act of psychic accommodation known as "intression."

At last Hagedorn spoke. "The castle is suddenly bereft of its Meks. Needless to say, this is an inconvenient condition to be adjusted as swiftly as possible. Here, I am sure, we find ourselves of one mind."

He looked around the table. All thrust forward carved ivory tablets to signify assent—all save Claghorn, who however did not stand it on end to signify dissent.

Isseth, a stern white-haired gentleman magnificently handsome in spite of his seventy years, spoke in a grim voice. "I see no point in cogitation or delay. What we must do is clear. Admittedly the Peasants are poor material from which to recruit an armed force. Nonetheless, we must assemble them, equip them with sandals, smocks and weapons so that they do not discredit us, and put them under good leadership: O.Z. Garr or Xanten. Birds can locate the vagrants, whereupon we will track them down, order the Peasants to give them a good drubbing, and herd them home on the double."

Xanten, thirty-five years old—extraordinarily

young to be a clan chief—and a notorious fire-brand, shook his head. "The idea is appealing but impractical. Peasants simply could not stand up to the Meks, no matter how we trained them."

The statement was manifestly accurate. The Peasants, small andromorphs originally of Spica Ten, were not so much timid as incapable of performing a vicious act.

A dour silence held the table. O.Z. Garr finally spoke. "The dogs have stolen our power-wagons, otherwise I'd be tempted to ride out and chivy the rascals home with a whip."*

"A matter of perplexity," said Hagedorn, "is syrup. Naturally they carried away what they could. When this is exhausted—what then? Will they starve? Impossible for them to return to their original diet. What was it? Swamp mud? Eh, Claghorn, you're the expert in these matters.

---

*This, only an approximate translation, fails to capture the pungency of the language. Several words have no contemporary equivalents. "Skirkling," as in "to send skirkling," denotes a frantic pell-mell flight in all directions, accompanied by a vibration or twinkling or jerking motion. To "volith" is to toy idly with a matter, the implication being that the person involved is of such Jovian potency that all difficulties dwindle to contemptible triviality. "Raudlebogs" are the semi-intelligent beings of Etamin Four, who were brought to Earth, trained first as gardeners, then construction laborers, then sent home in disgrace because of certain repulsive habits they refused to forgo.

The statement of O.Z. Garr, therefore, becomes something like this: "Were power-wagons at hand, I'd volith riding forth with a whip to send the raudlebogs skirkling home."

Can the Meks return to a diet of mud?"

"No," said Claghorn. "The organs of the adult are atrophied. If a cub were started on the diet, he'd probably survive."

"Just as I assumed." Hagedorn scowled portentously down at his clasped hands to conceal his total lack of any constructive proposal.

A gentleman in the dark blue of the Beaudrys appeared in the doorway: he poised himself, held high his right arm, and bowed so that the fingers swept the floor.

Hagedorn rose to his feet. "Come forward, B.F. Robarth; what is your news?" For this was the significance of the newcomer's genuflection.

"The news is a message broadcast from Halcyon. The Meks have attacked; they have fired the structure and are slaughtering all. The radio went dead one minute ago."

All swung around, some jumped to their feet. "Slaughter?" croaked Claghorn.

"I am certain that by now Halcyon is no more."

Claghorn sat staring with eyes unfocused. The others discussed the dire news in voices heavy with horror.

Hagedorn once more brought the council back to order. "This is clearly an extreme situation—the gravest, perhaps, of our entire history. I am frank to state that I can suggest no decisive counter-act."

Overwhele inquired, "What of the other

castles? Are they secure?"

Hagedorn turned to B.F. Robarth. "Will you be good enough to make general radio contact with all other castles, and inquire as to their condition?"

Xanten said, "Others are as vulnerable as Halcyon: Sea Island and Delora, in particular, and Maraval as well."

Claghorn emerged from his reverie. "The gentlemen and ladies of these places, in my opinion, should consider taking refuge at Janeil or here, until the uprising is quelled."

Others around the table looked at him in surprise and puzzlement. O.Z. Garr inquired in the silkiest of voices: "You envision the gentlefolk of these castles scampering to refuge at the cock-a-hoop swaggering of the lower orders?"

"Indeed, should they wish to survive," responded Claghorn politely. A gentleman of late middle age, Claghorn was stocky and strong, with black-gray hair, magnificent green eyes, and a manner which suggested great internal force under stern control. "Flight by definition entails a certain diminution of dignity," he went on to say. "If O.Z. Garr can propound an elegant manner of taking to one's heels, I will be glad to learn it, and everyone else should likewise heed, because in the days to come the capability may be of comfort to all."

Hagedorn interposed before O.Z. Garr could reply. "Let us keep to the issues. I confess I cannot see to the end of all this. The Meks have demonstrated themselves to be murderers; how can we take them back into our service? But if we don't—well, to say the least, conditions will be austere until we can locate and train a new force of technicians. We must consider along these lines."

"The spaceships!" exclaimed Xanten. "We must see to them at once!"

"What's this?" inquired Beaudry, a gentleman of rock-hard face. "How do you mean, 'see to them'?"

"They must be protected from damage! What else? They are our link to the Home Worlds. The maintenance Meks probably have not deserted the hangars, since, if they propose to exterminate us, they will want to deny us the spaceships."

"Perhaps you care to march with a levy of Peasants to take the hangars under firm control?" suggested O.Z. Garr in a somewhat supercilious voice. A long history of rivalry and mutual detestation existed between himself and Xanten.

"It may be our only hope," said Xanten. "Still —how does one fight with a levy of Peasants? Better that I fly to the hangars and reconnoiter. Meanwhile, perhaps you, and others with military expertise, will take in hand the recruitment and training of a Peasant militia."

"In this regard," stated O.Z. Garr, "I await

21

the outcome of our current deliberations. If it develops that there lies the optimum course, I naturally will apply my competences to the fullest degree. If your own capabilities are best fulfilled by spying out the activities of the Meks, I hope that you will be large-hearted enough to do the same."

The two gentlemen glared at each other. A year previously their enmity had almost culminated in a duel. Xanten, a gentleman tall, clean-limbed, and nervously active, was gifted with great natural flair, but likewise evinced a disposition too easy for absolute elegance. The traditionalists considered him "sthross," indicating a manner flawed by an almost imperceptible slackness and lack of punctilio: not the best possible choice for clan chief.

Xanten's response to O.Z. Garr was blandly polite. "I shall be glad to take this task upon myself. Since haste is of the essence I will risk the accusation of precipitousness and leave at once. Hopefully I return to report tomorrow." He rose, performed a ceremonious bow to Hagedorn, another all-inclusive salute to the council, and departed.

He crossed to Esledune House where he maintained an apartment on the thirteenth level: four rooms furnished in the style known as Fifth Dynasty, after an epoch in the history of the Altair Home Planets, from which the human race had returned to Earth. His current consort,

Araminta, a lady of the Onwane family, was absent on affairs of her own, which suited Xanten well enough. After plying him with questions she would have discredited his simple explanation, preferring to suspect an assignation at his country place. Truth to tell, he had become bored with Araminta and had reason to believe that she felt similarly—or perhaps his exalted rank had provided her less opportunity to preside at glittering social functions than she had expected. They had bred no children. Araminta's daughter by a previous connection had been tallied to her. Her second child must then be tallied to Xanten, preventing him from siring another child.*

Xanten doffed his yellow council vestments, and, assisted by a young Peasant buck, donned dark yellow hunting-breeches with black trim, a black jacket, black boots. He drew a cap of soft black leather over his head, and slung a pouch over his shoulder, into which he loaded weapons: a coiled blade, an energy gun.

Leaving the apartment, he summoned the lift and descended to the first level armory, where normally a Mek clerk would have served him. Now Xanten, to his vast disgust, was forced to

---

*The population of Castle Hagedorn was fixed; each gentleman and each lady was permitted a single child. If by chance another were born the parent must either find someone who had not yet sired to sponsor it, or dispose of it another way. The usual procedure was to give the child into the care of the Expiationists.

take himself behind the counter, and rummage here and there. The Meks had removed most of the sporting rifles, all the pellet ejectors and heavy energy-guns: an ominous circumstance, thought Xanten. At last he found a steel sling-whip, spare power slugs for his gun, a brace of fire grenades and a high-powered monocular.

He returned to the lift and rode to the top level, ruefully considering the long climb when eventually the mechanism broke down, with no Meks at hand to make repairs. He thought of the apoplectic furies of rigid traditionalists such as Beaudry and chuckled: eventful days lay ahead!

Stopping at the top level, he crossed to the parapets and proceeded around to the radio room. Customarily three Mek specialists connected into the apparatus by wires clipped to their quills sat typing messages as they arrived; now B.F. Robarth stood before the mechanism, uncertainly twisting the dials, his mouth wry with deprecation and distaste for the job.

"Any further news?" Xanten asked.

B.F. Robarth gave him a sour grin. "The folk at the other end seem no more familiar with this cursed tangle than I. I hear occasional voices. I believe that the Meks are attacking Castle Delora."

Claghorn had entered the room behind Xanten. "Did I hear you correctly? Delora Castle is gone?"

"Not gone yet, Claghorn. But as good as

gone. The Delora walls are little better than a picturesque crumble."

"Sickening situation!" muttered Xanten. "How can sentient creatures perform such evil? After all these centuries, how little we actually knew of them!" As he spoke he recognized the tactlessness of his remark; Claghorn had devoted much time to a study of the Meks.

"The act itself is not astounding," said Claghorn shortly. "It has occurred a thousand times in human history."

Mildly surprised that Claghorn should use human history in reference to a case involving the sub-orders, Xanten asked, "You were never aware of this vicious aspect to the Mek nature?"

"No. Never. Never indeed."

Claghorn seemed unduly sensitive, thought Xanten. Understandable, all in all. Claghorn's basic doctrine as set forth during the Hagedorn selection was by no means simple, and Xanten neither understood it nor completely endorsed what he conceived to be its goals; but it was plain that the revolt of the Meks had cut the ground out from under Claghorn's feet. Probably to the somewhat bitter satisfaction of O.Z. Garr, who must feel vindicated in his traditionalist doctrines.

Claghorn said tersely, "The life we've been leading couldn't last forever. It's a wonder it lasted as long as it did."

"Perhaps so," said Xanten in a soothing

25

voice. "Well, no matter. All things change. Who knows? The Peasants may be planning to poison our food. . . . I must go." He bowed to Claghorn, who returned him a crisp nod, and to B.F. Robarth, then departed the room.

He climbed the spiral staircase—almost a ladder—to the cotes, where the Birds lived in an invincible disorder, occupying themselves with gambling, quarrels, and a version of chess, with rules incomprehensible to every gentleman who had tried to understand it.

Castle Hagedorn maintained a hundred Birds, tended by a gang of long-suffering Peasants, whom the Birds held in vast disesteem. The Birds were garish garrulous creatures, pigmented red, yellow or blue, with long necks, jerking inquisitive heads and an inherent irreverence which no amount of discipline or tutelage could overcome. Spying Xanten, they emitted a chorus of rude jeers: "Somebody wants a ride! Heavy thing!" "Why don't the self-anointed two-footers grow wings for themselves?" "My friend, never trust a Bird! We'll sky you, then fling you down on your fundament!"

"Quiet!" called Xanten. "I need six fast silent Birds for an important mission. Are any capable of such a task?"

"Are any capable, he asks!" "*A ros ros!* When none of us have flown for a week!" "Silence? We'll give you silence, yellow and black!"

"Come then. You. You. You of the wise eye. You there. You with the cocked shoulder. You with the green pompon. To the basket."

The Birds designated, jeering, grumbling, reviling the Peasants, allowed their syrup sacs to be filled, then flapped to the wicker seat where Xanten waited. "To the space depot at Vincenne," he told them. "Fly high and silently. Enemies are abroad. We must learn what harm if any has been done to the spaceships."

"To the depot, then!" Each Bird seized a length of rope tied to an overhead framework; the chair was yanked up with a jerk calculated to rattle Xanten's teeth, and off they flew, laughing, cursing each other for not supporting more of the load, but eventually all accommodating themselves to the task and flying with a coordinated flapping of the thirty-six sets of wings. To Xanten's relief, their garrulity lessened; silently they flew south, at a speed of fifty or sixty miles per hour.

The afternoon was already waning. The ancient countryside, scene to so many comings and goings, so much triumph and so much disaster, was laced with long black shadows. Looking down, Xanten reflected that though the human stock was native to this soil, and though his immediate ancestors had maintained their holdings for seven hundred years, Earth still seemed an alien world. The reason of course was by no means mysterious or rooted in paradox. After the Six Star War, Earth had lain fallow for three thousand years, unpopulated save for a handful of anguished wretches who somehow had survived the cataclysm and who had become semi-barbaric Nomads. Then seven hundred years ago certain rich lords of Altair, motivated to some extent by political disaffection, but no less by caprice, had decided to return to Earth. Such was the origin of the nine great strongholds, the resident gentlefolk and the staffs of specialized andromorphs. . . . Xanten flew over an area where an antiquarian had directed excavations, revealing a plaza flagged with white stone, a broken obelisk, a tumbled statue. . . . The sight, by some trick of association, stimulated Xanten's mind to an astonishing vision, so simple and yet so grand that he looked around, in all directions, with new eyes. The vision was Earth re-populated with men, the land cultivated, Nomads driven back into the wilderness.

At the moment the image was farfetched. And Xanten, watching the soft contours of Old Earth slide below, pondered the Mek revolt which had altered his life with such startling abruptness.

Claghorn had long insisted that no human condition endured forever, with the corollary that the more complicated such a condition, the greater its susceptibility to change. In which case the seven hundred year continuity at Castle Hagedorn—as artificial, extravagant and intricate as life could be—became an astonishing circumstance in itself. Claghorn had pushed his thesis further. Since change was inevitable, he argued that the gentlefolk should soften the impact by anticipating and controlling the changes —a doctrine which had been attacked with great fervor. The traditionalists labeled all of Claghorn's ideas demonstrable fallacy, and cited the very stability of castle life as proof of its viability. Xanten had inclined first one way, then the other, emotionally involved with neither cause. If anything, the fact of O.Z. Garr's traditionalism had nudged him toward Claghorn's views, and now it seemed as if events had vindicated Claghorn. Change had come, with an impact of the maximum harshness and violence.

There were still questions to be answered, of course. Why had the Meks chosen this particular time to revolt? Conditions had not altered appreciably for five hundred years, and the Meks had never previously hinted dissatisfaction. In fact they had revealed nothing of their feelings, though no one had ever troubled to ask them— save Claghorn.

The Birds were veering east to avoid the Ballarat Mountains, to the west of which were the ruins of a great city, never satisfactorily identified. Below lay the Lucerne Valley, at one time a fertile farm land. If one looked with great concentration, the outline of the various holdings could sometimes be distinguished. Ahead, the spaceship hangars were visible, where Mek technicians maintained four spaceships jointly the property of Hagedorn, Janeil, Tuang, Morninglight and Maraval, though, for a variety of reasons, the ships were never used.

The sun was setting. Orange light twinkled and flickered on the metal walls. Xanten called instructions up to the Birds: "Circle down. Alight behind that line of trees, but fly low so that none will see."

Down on stiff wings curved the Birds, six ungainly necks stretched toward the ground. Xanten was ready for the impact; the Birds never seemed able to alight easily when they carried a gentleman. When the cargo was something in which they felt a personal concern, dandelion fluff would never have been disturbed by the jar.

Xanten expertly kept his balance, instead of tumbling and rolling in the manner preferred by the Birds. "You all have syrup," he told them. "Rest; make no noise; do not quarrel. By tomorrow's sunset, if I am not here, return to Castle Hagedorn and say that Xanten was killed."

"Never fear!" cried the Birds. "We will wait forever!" "At any rate till tomorrow's sunset!" "If danger threatens, if you are pressed—*a ros ros ros!* Call for the Birds!" "*A ros!* We are ferocious when aroused!"

"I wish it were true," said Xanten. "The Birds are arrant cowards; this is well-known. Still I value the sentiment. Remember my instructions, and quiet above all! I do not wish to be set upon and stabbed because of your clamor."

The Birds made indignant sounds. "Injustice, injustice! We are quiet as the dew!"

"Good." Xantan hurriedly moved away lest they should bellow new advice or reassurances after him.

Passing through the forest, he came to an open meadow at the far edge of which, perhaps a hundred yards distant, was the rear of the first hangar. He stopped to consider. Several factors were involved. First: the maintenance Meks, with the metal structure shielding them from radio contact, might still be unaware of the revolt. Hardly likely, he decided, in view of the otherwise careful planning. Second: the Meks, in continuous communication with their fellows, acted as a collective organism. The aggregate functioned more competently than its parts, and the individual was not prone to initiative. Hence, vigilance was likely to be extreme. Third: if they expected anyone to attempt a discreet approach, they would necessarily scrutinize most closely the route which he proposed to take.

Xanten decided to wait in the shadows another ten minutes, until the setting sun shining over his shoulder should most effectively blind any who might watch.

Ten minutes passed. The hangars, burnished by the dying sunlight, bulked long, tall, completely quiet. In the intervening meadow long

31

golden grass waved and rippled in a cool breeze. . . . Xanten took a deep breath, hefted his pouch, arranged his weapons, and strode forth. It did not occur to him to crawl through the grass.

He reached the back of the nearest hangar without challenge. Pressing his ear to the metal he heard nothing. He walked to the corner, looked down the side: no sign of life. Xanten shrugged: very well, then; to the door.

He walked beside the hangar, the setting sun casting a long black shadow ahead of him. He came to a door opening into the hangar administrative office. Since there was nothing to be gained by trepidation, Xanten thrust the door aside and entered.

The offices were empty. The desks, where centuries before underlings had sat, calculating invoices and bills of lading, were bare, polished free of dust. The computers and information banks, black enamel, glass, white and red switches, looked as if they had been installed only the day before.

Xanten crossed to the glass pane overlooking the hangar floor, shadowed under the bulk of the ship.

He saw no Meks. But on the floor of the hangar, arranged in neat rows and heaps, were elements and assemblies of the ship's control mechanism. Service panels gaped wide into the hull to show where the devices had been detached.

Xanten stepped from the office out into the hangar. The spaceship had been disabled, put out of commission. Xanten looked along the neat rows of parts. Certain savants of various castles were expert in the theory of space-time transfer; S.X. Rosenbox of Maraval had even derived a set of equations which, if translated into machinery, eliminated the troublesome Hamus effect. But not one gentleman, even were he so oblivious to personal honor as to touch a hand to a tool, would know how to replace, connect and tune the mechanisms heaped upon the hangar floor.

The malicious work had been done—when? Impossible to say.

Xanten returned to the office, stepped back out into the twilight, and walked to the next hangar. Again no Meks; again the spaceship had been gutted of its control mechanisms. Xanten proceeded to the third hangar, where conditions were the same.

At the fourth hangar he discerned the faint sounds of activity. Stepping into the office, looking through the glass wall into the hangar, he found Meks working with their usual economy of motion, in a near silence which was uncanny.

Xanten, already uncomfortable from skulking through the forest, became enraged by the cool destruction of his property. He strode forth into the hangar. Slapping his thigh to attract attention he called in a harsh voice, "Return the components to place! How dare you vermin act in such a manner?"

The Meks turned about their blank countenances to study him through black beaded lens clusters at each side of their heads.

"What?" bellowed Xanten. "You hesitate?" He brought forth his steel whip, usually more of a symbolic adjunct than a punitive instrument, and slashed it against the ground. "Obey! This ridiculous revolt is at its end!"

The Meks still hesitated, and events wavered in the balance. None made a sound, though messages were passing among them, appraising the circumstances, establishing a consensus. Xanten could allow them no such leisure. He marched forward, wielding the whip, striking at the only area where the Meks felt pain: the ropy face. "To your duties," he roared. "A fine maintenance crew are you! A destruction crew is more like it!"

The Meks made the soft blowing sound which might mean anything. They fell back, and now Xanten noted one standing at the head of the companionway leading into the ship: a Mek larger than any he had seen before and one in some fashion different. This Mek was aiming a pellet gun at his head. With an unhurried flourish, Xanten whipped away a Mek who had leaped forward with a knife, and without deigning to aim, fired at and destroyed the Mek who stood on the companionway, even as the slug sang past his head.

The other Meks were nevertheless committed to an attack. All surged forward. Lounging disdainfully against the hull, Xanten shot them as they came, moving his head once to avoid a chunk of metal, again reaching to catch a throwknife and hurl it into the face of him who had thrown it.

The Meks drew back, and Xanten guessed that they had agreed on a new tactic; either to withdraw for weapons or perhaps to confine him within the hangar. In any event no more could be accomplished here. He made play with the whip and cleared an avenue to the office. With tools, metal bars and forgings striking the glass behind him, he sauntered through the office and out into the night.

The full moon was rising: a great yellow globe casting a smoky saffron glow, like an antique lamp. Mek eyes were not well-adapted for nightseeing, and Xanten waited by the door. Presently Meks began to pour forth, and Xanten hacked at their necks as they came.

The Meks drew back inside the hangar. Wiping his blade, Xanten strode off the way he had come, looking neither right nor left. He stopped short. The night was young. Something tickled his mind: the recollection of the Mek who had fired the pellet gun. He had been larger, possibly a darker bronze, but, more significantly, he had displayed an indefinable poise, almost authority —though such a word, when used in connection with the Meks, was anomalous. On the other hand, someone must have planned the revolt, or at least originated the concept. It might be worthwhile to extend the reconnaissance, though his primary information had been secured.

Xanten turned back and crossed the landing area to the barracks and garages. Once more, frowning in discomfort, he felt the need for discretion. What times these were! when a gentleman must skulk to avoid such as the Meks! He stole up behind the garages, where a half-dozen power-wagons* lay dozing.

Xanten looked them over. All were of the same sort, a metal frame with four wheels, an earth-moving blade at the front. Nearby must be the syrup stock. Xanten presently found a bin containing a number of containers. He loaded a dozen on a nearby wagon, slashed the rest with his knife, so that the syrup gushed across the ground. The Meks used a somewhat different

---

*Power-wagons, like the Meks, originally swamp-creatures from Etamin 9, were great rectangular slabs of muscle, slung into a rectangular frame and protected from sunlight, insects and rodents by a synthetic pelt. Syrup sacs communicated with their digestive apparatus, wires led to motor nodes in the rudimentary brain. The muscles were clamped to rocker arms which actuated rotors and drive-wheels. The power-wagons, economical, long-lived, and docile, were principally used for heavy cartage, earth-moving, heavy-tillage, and other arduous jobs.

formulation; their syrup would be stocked at a different locale, presumably inside the barracks.

Xanten mounted a power-wagon, twisted the *awake* key, tapped the *go* button, and pulled a lever which set the wheels into reverse motion. The power-wagon lurched back. Xanten halted it, turned it so that it faced the barracks. He did likewise with three others, then set them all into motion, one after the other. They trundled forward; the blades cut open the metal wall of the barracks, the roof sagged. The power-wagons continued, pushing the length of the interior, crushing all in their way.

Xanten nodded in profound satisfaction and returned to the power-wagon he had reserved for his own use. Mounting to the seat, he waited. No Meks issued from the barracks. Apparently they were deserted, with the entire crew busy at the hangars. Still, hopefully, the syrup stocks had been destroyed, and many might perish by starvation.

From the direction of the hangars came a single Mek, evidently attracted by the sounds of destruction. Xanten crouched on the seat and as it passed, coiled his whip around the stock neck. He heaved; the Mek spun to the ground.

Xanten leaped down, seized its pellet-gun. Here was another of the larger Meks, and now Xanten saw it to be without a syrup sac, a Mek in the original state. Astounding! How did the creature survive? Suddenly there were many new questions to be asked—hopefully a few to be answered. Standing on the creature's head, Xanten hacked away the long antenna quills which protruded from the back of the Mek's scalp. It was now insulated, alone, on its own resources—a situation to reduce the most stalwart Mek to apathy.

"Up!" ordered Xanten. "Into the back of the wagon!" He cracked the whip for emphasis.

The Mek at first seemed disposed to defy him, but after a blow or two obeyed. Xanten climbed into the seat and started the power-wagon, directed it to the north. The Birds would be unable to carry both himself and the Mek—or in any event they would cry and complain so raucously that they might as well be believed at first. They might or might not wait until the specified hour of tomorrow's sunset; as likely as not they would sleep the night in a tree, awake in a surly mood and return at once to Castle Hagedorn.

All through the night the power-wagon trundled, with Xanten on the seat and his captive huddled in the rear.

CHAPTER THREE

1

The gentlefolk of the castles, for all their assurance, disliked to wander the countryside by night, by reason of what some derided as superstitious fear. Others cited travelers benighted beside moldering ruins and their subsequent visions: the eldritch music they had heard, or the whimper of moon-mirkins, or the far horns of spectral huntsmen. Others had seen pale lavender and green lights, and wraiths which ran with long strides through the forest; and Hode Abbey, now a dank tumble, was notorious for the White Hag and the alarming toll she exacted.

A hundred such cases were known, and while the hardheaded scoffed, none needlessly traveled the countryside by night. Indeed, if ghosts truly haunt the scenes of tragedy and heartbreak, then the landscape of Old Earth must be home to ghosts and specters beyond all numbering—especially that region across which Xanten rolled in the power-wagon, where every rock, every meadow, every vale and swale was crusted thick with human experience.

The moon rose high; the wagon trundled north along an ancient road, the cracked concrete slabs shining pale in the moonlight. Twice Xanten saw flickering orange lights off to the side, and once, standing in the shade of a cypress tree, he thought he saw a tall, quiet shape, silently watching him pass. The captive Mek sat plotting mischief, Xanten well knew. Without its quills it must feel depersonified, bewildered, but Xanten told himself that it would not do to doze.

The road led through a town, certain structures of which still stood. Not even the Nomads took refuge in these old towns, fearing either miasma or perhaps the redolence of grief.

The moon reached the zenith. The landscape spread away in a hundred tones of silver, black and gray. Looking about, Xanten thought that for all the notable pleasures of civilized life, there was yet something to be said for the spaciousness and simplicity of Nomadland. The Mek made a stealthy movement. Xanten did not so much as turn his head. He cracked his whip in the air. The Mek became quiet.

All through the night the power-wagon rolled along the old road, with the moon sinking into the west. The eastern horizon glowed green and lemon-yellow, and presently, as the pallid moon disappeared, the sun rose over the distant line of the mountains. At this moment, off to the right, Xanten spied a drift of smoke.

He halted the wagon. Standing up on the seat, he craned his neck to spy a Nomad encampment about a quarter-mile distant. He could distinguish three or four dozen tents of various sizes and a dozen dilapidated power-wagons. On the hetman's tall tent he thought he saw a black ideogram that he recognized. If so, this would be the tribe which not long before had trespassed on the Hagedorn domain, and which O.Z. Garr had repulsed.

Xanten settled himself upon the seat, composed his garments, set the power-wagon in motion, and guided it toward the camp.

A hundred black-cloaked men, tall and lean as ferrets, watched his approach. A dozen sprang forward and whipping arrows to bows, aimed them at his heart. Xanten turned them a glance of supercilious inquiry, drove the wagon up to the hetman's tent, halted. He rose to his feet. "Hetman," he called. "Are you awake?"

The hetman parted the canvas which closed off his tent, peered out, and after a moment came forth. Like the others he wore a garment of limp black cloth, swathing head and body alike. His face thrust through a square opening: narrow blue eyes, a grotesquely long nose, a chin long, skewed and sharp.

Xanten gave him a curt nod. "Observe this."

He jerked his thumb toward the Mek in the back of the wagon. The hetman flicked aside his eyes, studied the Mek a tenth-second, and returned to a scrutiny of Xanten. "His kind have revolted against the gentlemen," said Xanten. "In fact they massacre all the men of Earth. Hence we of Castle Hagedorn make this offer to the Nomads. Come to Castle Hagedorn. We will feed, clothe and arm you. We will train you to discipline and the arts of formal warfare. We will provide the most expert leadership within our power. We will then annihilate the Meks, expunge them from Earth. After the campaign, we will train you to technical skills, and you may pursue profitable and interesting careers in the service of the castles."

The hetman made no reply for a moment. Then his weathered face split into a ferocious grin. He spoke in a voice which Xanten found surprisingly well-modulated. "So your beasts have finally risen up to rend you! A pity they forebore so long! Well, it is all one to us. You are both alien folk and sooner or later your bones must bleach together."

Xanten pretended incomprehension. "If I understand you aright, you assert that in the face of alien assault, all men must fight a common battle; and then, after the victory, cooperate still to their mutual advantage. Am I correct?"

The hetman's grin never wavered. "You are not men. Only we of Earth soil and Earth water

43

are men. You and your weird slaves are strangers together. We wish you success in your mutual slaughter."

"Well, then," declared Xanten, "I heard you aright after all. Appeals to your loyalty are ineffectual, so much is clear. What of self-interest, then? The Meks, failing to expunge the gentlefolk of the castles, will turn upon the Nomads and kill them as if they were so many ants."

"If they attack us, we will war on them," said the hetman. "Otherwise let them do as they will."

Xanten glanced thoughtfully at the sky. "We might be willing, even now, to accept a contingent of Nomads into the service of Castle Hagedorn, this to form a cadre from which a larger, more versatile, group may be formed."

From the side, another Nomad called in an offensively jeering voice, "You will sew a sac on our backs where you can pour your syrup, hey?"

Xanten replied in an even voice, "The syrup is highly nutritious and supplies all bodily needs."

"Why then do you not consume it yourself?"

Xanten disdained reply.

The hetman spoke. "If you wish to supply us weapons, we will take them, and use them against whomever threatens us. But do not expect us to defend you. If you fear for your lives, desert your castles and become Nomads."

"Fear for our lives?" exclaimed Xanten. "What nonsense! Never! Castle Hagedorn is im-

44

pregnable, as is Janeil, and most of the other castles as well."

The hetman shook his head. "Any time we choose we could take Hagedorn, and kill all you popinjays in your sleep."

"What?" cried Xanten in outrage. "Are you serious?"

"Certainly. On a black night we would send a man aloft on a great kite and drop him down on the parapets. He would lower a line, haul up ladders and in fifteen minutes the castle is taken."

Xanten pulled at his chin. "Ingenious, but impractical. The Birds would detect such a kite. Or the wind would fail at a critical moment. . . . All this is beside the point. The Meks fly no kites. They plan to make a display against Janeil and Hagedorn, then, in their frustration, go forth and hunt Nomads."

The hetman moved back a step. "What then? We have survived similar attempts by the men of Hagedorn. Cowards all. Hand to hand, with equal weapons, we would make you eat the dirt like the dogs you are."

Xanten raised his eyebrows in elegant disdain. "I fear that you forget yourself. You address a clan chief of Castle Hagedorn. Only fatigue and boredom restrain me from punishing you with this whip."

"Bah," said the hetman. He crooked a finger to one of his archers. "Spit this insolent lordling."

The archer discharged his arrow, but Xanten, who had been expecting some such act, fired his energy gun, destroying arrow, bow, and the archer's hands. He said, "I see I must teach you common respect for your betters; so it means the whip after all." Seizing the hetman by the scalp, he coiled the whip smartly once, twice, thrice around the narrow shoulders. "Let this suffice. I cannot compel you to fight, but at least I can demand decent respect." He leaped to the ground, and seizing the hetman, pitched him into the back of the wagon alongside the Mek. Then, backing the power-wagon around, he departed the camp without so much as a glance over his shoulder, the thwart of the seat protecting his back from arrows.

The hetman scrambled erect, drew his dagger. Xanten turned his head slightly. "Take care! Or I will tie you to the wagon and you shall run behind in the dust."

The hetman hesitated, made a spitting sound between his teeth, drew back. He looked down at his blade, turned it over, and sheathed it with a grunt. "Where do you take me?"

Xanten halted the wagon. "No farther. I merely wished to leave your camp with dignity, without dodging and ducking a hail of arrows. You may alight. I take it you still refuse to bring your men into the service of Castle Hagedorn?"

The hetman once more made the spitting sound between his teeth. "When the Meks have destroyed the castles, we shall destroy the Meks, and Earth will be cleared of star-things."

"You are a gang of intractable savages. Very well, alight, return to your encampment. Reflect well before you again show disrespect to a Castle Hagedorn clan chief."

"Bah," muttered the hetman. Leaping down from the wagon, he stalked back down the track toward his camp.

2

About noon Xanten came to Far Valley, at the edge of the Hagedorn lands. Nearby was a village of Expiationists: malcontents and neurasthenics in the opinion of castle gentlefolk, and a curious group by any standards. A few had held enviable rank; certain others were savants of recognized erudition; but others yet were persons of neither dignity nor reputation, subscribing to the most bizarre and extreme of philosophies. All now performed toil no different from that relegated to the Peasants, and all seemed to take a perverse satisfaction in what —by castle standards—was filth, poverty and degradation.

As might be expected, their creed was by no means homogeneous. Some might better have been described as "nonconformists" or "disassociationists"; another group were "passive expiationists," and others still, a minority, argued for a dynamic program.

Between castle and village was little intercourse. Occasionally the Expiationists bartered fruit or polished wood for tools, nails, medicaments; or the gentlefolk might make up a party to watch the Expiationists at their dancing and singing. Xanten had visited the village on many such occasions and had been attracted by the artless charm and informality of the folk at their play. Now, passing near the village, Xanten turned aside to follow a lane which wound between tall blackberry hedges and out upon a little common where goats and cattle grazed. Xanten halted the wagon in the shade and saw that the syrup sac was full. He looked back at his captive. "What of you? If you need syrup, pour yourself full. But no, you have no sac. What then do you feed upon? Mud? Unsavory fare. I fear none here is rank enough for your taste. Ingest syrup or munch grass, as you will; only do not stray overfar from the wagon, for I watch with an intent eye."

The Mek, sitting hunched in a corner, gave no signal that it comprehended, nor did it move to take advantage of Xanten's offer.

Xanten went to a watering trough and holding his hands under the trickle which issued from a lead pipe, rinsed his face, then drank a swallow or two from his cupped hand.

Turning, he found that a dozen folk of the village had approached. One he knew well, a man who might have become Godalming, or even Aure, had he not become infected with expiationism.

Xanten performed a polite salute, "A.G. Philidor: it is I, Xanten."

"Xanten, of course. But here I am A.G. Philidor no longer, merely Philidor."

Xanten bowed. "My apologies; I have neglected the full rigor of your informality."

"Spare me your wit," said Philidor. "Why do you bring us a shorn Mek? For adoption, perhaps?" This last alluded to the gentlefolk practice of bringing over-tally babies to the village.

"Now who flaunts his wit? But you have not heard the news?"

"News arrives here last of all. The Nomads are better informed."

"Prepare yourself for surprise. The Meks have revolted against the castles. Halcyon and Delora are demolished, and all killed; perhaps others by this time."

Philidor shook his head. "I am not surprised."

"Well then, are you not concerned?"

Philidor considered. "To this extent. Our own plans, never very feasible, become more farfetched than ever."

"It appears to me," said Xanten, "that you face grave and immediate danger. The Meks surely intend to wipe out every vestige of humanity. You will not escape."

Philidor shrugged. "Conceivably the danger exists. . . . We will take counsel and decide what to do."

"I can put forward a proposal which you may find attractive," said Xanten. "Our first concern, of course, is to suppress the revolt. There are at least a dozen Expiationist communities, with an aggregate population of two or three thousand—perhaps more. I propose that we recruit and train a corps of highly disciplined troops, supplied from the Castle Hagedorn armory, led by Hagedorn's most expert military theoreticians."

Philidor stared at him incredulously. "You expect us, the Expiationists, to become your soldiers?"

"Why not?" asked Xanten ingenuously. "Your life is at stake no less than ours."

"No one dies more than once."

Xanten in his turn evinced shock. "What? Can this be a former gentleman of Hagedorn speaking? Is this the face a man of pride and courage turns to danger? Is this the lesson of history? Of course not! I need not instruct you in this; you are as knowledgeable as I."

Philidor nodded. "I know that the history of man is not his technical triumphs, his kills, his victories. It is a composite, a mosaic of a trillion pieces, the account of each man's accommoda-

50

tion with his conscience. This is the true history of the race."

Xanten made an airy gesture. "A.G. Philidor, you oversimplify grievously. Do you consider me obtuse? There are many kinds of history. They interact. You emphasize morality. But the ultimate basis of morality is survival. What promotes survival is good, what induces mortification is bad."

"Well spoken!" declared Philidor. "But let me propound a parable. May a nation of a million beings destroy a creature who otherwise will infect all with a fatal disease? Yes, you will say. Once more: ten starving beasts hunt you, that they may eat. Will you kill them to save your life? Yes, you will say again, though here you destroy more than you save. Once more: a man inhabits a hut in a lonely valley. A hundred spaceships descend from the sky, and attempt to destroy him. May he destroy these ships in self-defense, even though he is one and they are a hundred thousand? Perhaps you say yes. What then if a whole world, a whole race of beings, pits itself against this single man? May he kill all? What if the attackers are as human as himself? What if he were the creature of the first instance, who otherwise will infect a world with disease? You see, there is no area where a simple touchstone avails. We have searched and found none. Hence, at the risk of sinning against Survival, we—I, at least; I can only speak for myself

—have chosen a morality which at least allows me calm. I kill—nothing. I destroy—nothing."

"Bah," said Xanten contemptuously. "If a Mek platoon entered this valley and began to kill your children, you would not defend them?"

Philidor compressed his lips, turned away. Another man spoke. "Philidor has defined morality. But who is absolutely moral? Philidor, or I, or you, might desert his morality in such a case."

Philidor said, "Look about you. Is there anyone here you recognize?"

Xanten scanned the group. Nearby stood a girl of extraordinary beauty. She wore a white smock and in the dark hair curling to her shoulders she wore a red flower. Xanten nodded. "I see the maiden O.Z. Garr wished to introduce into his ménage at the castle."

"Exactly," said Philidor. "Do you recall the circumstances?"

"Very well indeed," said Xanten. "There was vigorous objection from the Council of Notables —if for no other reason than the threat to our laws of population control. O.Z. Garr attempted to sidestep the law in this fashion. 'I keep Phanes,' he said. 'At times I maintain as many as six, or even eight, and no one utters a word of protest. I will call this girl Phane and keep her among the rest.' I and others protested. There was almost a duel over this matter. O.Z. Garr was forced to relinquish the girl. She was given

52

into my custody and I conveyed her to Far Valley."

Philidor nodded. "All this is correct. Well—we attempted to dissuade Garr. He refused to be dissuaded, and threatened us with his hunting force of perhaps thirty Meks. We stood aside. Are we moral? Are we strong or weak?"

"Sometimes it is better," said Xanten, "to ignore morality. Even though O.Z. Garr is a gentleman and you are but Expiationists. . . . Likewise in the case of the Meks. They are destroying the castles, and all the men of Earth. If morality means supine acceptance, then morality must be abandoned!"

Philidor gave a sour chuckle. "What a remarkable situation! The Meks are here, likewise Peasants and Birds and Phanes, all altered, transported and enslaved for human pleasure. Indeed, it is this fact that occasions our guilt, for which we must expiate, and now you want us to compound this guilt!"

"It is a mistake to brood overmuch about the past," said Xanten. "Still, if you wish to preserve your option to brood, I suggest that you fight Meks now, or at the very least take refuge in the castle."

"Not I," said Philidor. "Perhaps others may choose to do so."

"You will wait to be killed?"

"No. I and no doubt others will take refuge in the remote mountains."

Xanten clambered back aboard the power-wagon. "If you change your mind, come to Castle Hagedorn."

He departed.

The road continued along the valley, wound up a hillside, crossed a ridge. Far ahead, silhouetted against the sky, stood Castle Hagedorn.

CHAPTER FOUR

1

Xanten reported to the council.

"The spaceships cannot be used. The Meks have rendered them inoperative. Any plan to solicit assistance from the Home Worlds is pointless."

"This is sorry news," said Hagedorn with a grimace. "Well, then—so much for that."

Xanten continued. "Returning by power-wagon I encountered a tribe of Nomads. I summoned the hetman and explained to him the advantages of serving Castle Hagedorn. The Nomads, I fear, lack both grace and docility. The hetman gave so surly a response that I departed in disgust.

"At Far Valley I visited the Expiationist village, and made a similar proposal, but with no great success. They are as idealistic as the Nomads are churlish. Both are of a fugitive tendency. The Expiationists spoke of taking refuge in the mountains. The Nomads presumably will retreat into the steppes."

Beaudry snorted. "How will flight help them? Perhaps they gain a few years—but eventually the Meks will find every last one of them; such as their methodicity."

"In the meantime," O.Z. Garr declared peevishly, "we might have organized them into an efficient combat corps, to the benefit of all. Well, then, let them perish; we are secure."

"Secure, yes," said Hagedorn gloomily. "But what when the power fails? When the lifts break down? When air circulation cuts off so that we either stifle or freeze? What then?"

O.Z. Garr gave his head a grim shake. "We must steel ourselves to undignified expedients, with as good grace as possible. But the machinery of the castle is sound, and I expect small deterioration or failure for conceivably five or ten years. By that time anything may occur."

Claghorn, who had been leaning indolently back in his seat, spoke at last: "This essentially is a passive program. Like the defection of the Nomads and Expiationists, it looks very little beyond the immediate moment."

O.Z. Garr spoke in a voice carefully polite. "Claghorn is well aware that I yield to none in courteous candor, as well as optimism and directness: in short the reverse of passivity. But I refuse to dignify a stupid little inconvenience by extending it serious attention. How can he label this procedure passivity? Does the worthy and honorable head of the Claghorns have a proposal which more effectively maintains our status, our standards, our self-respect?"

Claghorn nodded slowly, with a faint half-smile which O.Z. Garr found odiously complacent. "There is a simple and effective method by which the Meks might be defeated."

"Well, then!" cried Hagedorn. "Why hesitate? Let us hear it!"

Claghorn looked around the red velvet-covered table, considering the faces of all: the dispassionate Xanten; Beaudry, burly, rigid, face muscles clenched in an habitual expression unpleasantly like a sneer; old Isseth, as handsome, erect and vital as the most dashing cadet; Hagedorn, troubled, glum, his inward perplexity all too evident; the elegant Garr; Overwhele, thinking savagely of the inconveniences of the future; Aure, toying with his ivory tablet, either bored, morose or defeated; the others displaying various aspects of doubt, foreboding, hauteur, dark resentment, impatience; and in the case of Floy, a quiet smile—or as Isseth later characterized it, an imbecilic smirk—intended to convey his total disassociation from the entire irksome matter.

Claghorn took stock of the faces, and shook his head. "I will not at the moment broach this plan, as I fear it is unworkable. But I must point out that under no circumstances can Castle Hagedorn be as before, even should we survive the Mek attack."

"Bah!" exclaimed Beaudry. "We loose dignity, we become ridiculous, by even so much as discussing the beasts."

Xanten stirred himself. "A distasteful subject, but remember! Halcyon is destroyed, and Delora, and who knows what others? Let us not thrust our heads in the sand! The Meks will not waft away merely because we ignore them."

"In any event," said O.Z. Garr, "Janeil is secure and we are secure. The other folk, unless they are already slaughtered, might do well to visit us during the inconvenience, if they can justify the humiliation of flight to themselves. I myself believe that the Meks will soon come to heel, anxious to return to their posts."

Hagedorn shook his head gloomily. "I find this hard to believe. But very well then, we shall adjourn."

2

The radio communication system was the first of the castle's vast array of electrical and mechanical devices to break down. The failure occurred so soon and so decisively that certain of the theoreticians, notably I.K. Harde and

Uegus, postulated sabotage by the departing
Meks. Others remarked that the system had never been absolutely dependable, that the Meks
themselves had been forced to tinker continuously with the circuits, that the failure was
simply a result of faulty engineering. I.K. Harde
and Uegus inspected the unwieldy apparatus,
but the cause of failure was not obvious. After a
half-hour of consultation they agreed that any
attempt to restore the system would necessitate
complete re-design and re-engineering, with con-
sequent construction of testing and calibration
devices, and the fabrication of a completely new
family of components. "This is manfestly impossible," stated Uegus in his report to the council. "Even the simplest useful system would re-
quire several technician-years. There is not even
one single technician to hand. We must therefore
await the availability of trained and willing labor."

"In retrospect," stated Isseth, the oldest of the
clan chiefs, "it is clear that in many ways we
have been less than provident. No matter that
the men of the Home Worlds are vulgarians!
Men of shrewder calculation than our own
would have maintained interworld connection."

"Lack of shrewdness and providence were not
the deterring factors," stated Claghorn. "Communication was discouraged simply because the
early lords were unwilling that Earth should be

overrun with Home-World parvenus. It is as simple as that."

Isseth grunted, and started to make a rejoinder, but Hagedorn said hastily, "Unluckily, as Xanten tells us, the spaceships have been rendered useless, and while certain of our number have a profound knowledge of the theoretical considerations, again who is there to perform the toil? Even were the hangars and spaceships themselves under our control."

O.Z. Garr declared, "Give me six platoons of Peasants and six power-wagons equipped with high-energy cannon, and I'll regain the hangars; no difficulties there!"

Beaudry said, "Well, here's a start, at least. I'll assist in the training of the Peasants, and though I know nothing of cannon operation, rely on me for any advice I can give."

Hagedorn looked around the group, frowned, pulled at his chin. "There are difficulties to this program. First, we have at hand only the single power-wagon in which Xanten returned from his reconnaissance. Then, what of our energy cannons? Has anyone inspected them? The Meks were entrusted with maintenance, but it is possible, even likely, that they wrought mischief here as well. O.Z. Garr, you are reckoned an expert military theoretician; what can you tell us in this regard?"

"I have made no inspection to date," stated O.Z. Garr. "Today the Display of Antique

Tabards will occupy us all until the Hour of Sundown Appraisal*." He looked at his watch. "Perhaps now is as good as time as any to adjourn, until I am able to provide detailed information in regard to the cannons."

Hagedorn nodded his heavy head. "The time indeed grows late. Your Phanes appear today?"

"Only two," replied O.Z. Garr. "The Lazule and the Eleventh Mystery. I can find nothing suitable for the Gossamer Delights nor my little Blue Fay, and the Gloriana still requires tutelage. Today B.Z. Maxelwane's Variflors should repay the most attention."

"Yes," said Hagedorn. "I have heard other remarks to this effect. Very well, then, until tomorrow. Eh, Claghorn, you have something to say?"

"Yes, indeed," said Claghorn mildly. "We have all too little time at our disposal. Best that we make the most of it. I seriously doubt the efficacy of Peasant troops; to pit Peasants against Meks is like sending rabbits against wolves. What we need, rather than rabbits, are panthers."

"Ah, yes," said Hagedorn vaguely. "Yes, indeed."

"Where, then, are panthers to be found?"

---

*Display of Antique Tabards; Hour of Sundown Appraisal: the literal sense of the first term was yet relevant; that of the second had become lost and the phrase was a mere formalism, connoting that hour of late afternoon when visits were exchanged, and wines, liqueurs and essences tasted: in short, a time of relaxation and small talk before the more formal convivialities of dining.

Claghorn looked inquiringly around the table. "Can no one suggest a source? A pity. Well then, if panthers fail to appear, I suppose rabbits must do. Let us go about the business of converting rabbits into panthers, and instantly. I suggest that we postpone all fetes and spectacles until the shape of our future is more certain."

Hagedorn raised his eyebrows, opened his mouth to speak, closed it again. He looked intently at Claghorn to ascertain whether or not he joked. Then he looked dubiously around the table.

Beaudry gave a rather brassy laugh. "It seems that erudite Claghorn cries panic."

O.Z. Garr stated: "Surely, in all dignity, we cannot allow the impertinence of our servants to cause us such eye-rolling alarm. I am embarrassed even to bring the matter forward."

"I am not embarrassed," said Claghorn, with the full-faced complacence which so exasperated O.Z. Garr. "I see no reason why you should be. Our lives are threatened, in which case a trifle of embarrassment, or anything else, becomes of secondary importance."

O.Z. Garr rose to his feet, performed a brusque salute in Claghorn's direction, of such a nature as to constitute a calculated affront. Claghorn, rising, performed a similar salute, so grave and overly complicated as to invest Garr's insult with burlesque overtones. Xanten, who detested O.Z. Garr, laughed aloud.

O.Z. Garr hesitated, then, sensing that under the circumstances taking the matter further would be regarded as poor form, strode from the chamber.

3

The Viewing of Antique Tabards, an annual pageant of Phanes wearing sumptuous garments, took place in the Great Rotunda to the north of the central plaza. Possibly half of the gentlemen, but less than a quarter of the ladies, kept Phanes. These were creatures native to the caverns of Albireo Seven's moon: a docile race, both playful and affectionate, which after several thousand years of selective breeding had become sylphs of piquant beauty. Clad in a delicate gauze which issued from pores behind their ears, along their upper arms and down their backs, they were the most inoffensive of creatures, anxious always to please, innocently vain. Most gentlemen regarded them with affection, but rumors sometimes told of ladies drenching an especially hated Phane in tincture of ammonia, which matted her pelt and destroyed her gauze forever.

A gentleman besotted by a Phane was considered a figure of fun. The Phane, though so carefully bred as to seem a delicate girl, if used sexually became crumpled and haggard, with gauzes drooping and discolored, and everyone would know that such and such a gentleman had misused his Phane. In this regard, at least, the women of the castles might exert their superiority, and did so by conducting themselves with such extravagant provocation that the Phanes in contrast seemed the most ingenious and fragile of nature sprites. Their life span was perhaps thirty years, during the last ten of which, after they had lost their beauty, they encased themselves in mantles of gray gauze and performed menial tasks in boudoirs, kitchens, pantries, nurseries and dressing rooms.

The Viewing of Antique Tabards was an occasion more for the viewing of Phanes than the tabards, though these, woven of Phane-gauze, were of great intrinsic beauty in themselves.

The Phane owners sat in a lower tier, tense with hope and pride, exulting when one made an especially splendid display, plunging into black depths when the ritual postures were performed with other than grace and elegance. During each display, highly formal music was plucked from a lute by a gentleman from a clan different to that of the Phane owner, the owner never playing the lute to the performance of his own Phane. The display was never overtly a competition and no formal acclamation was allowed, but all watching made up their minds as to which was the most entrancing and graceful of the Phanes, and the repute of the owner was thereby exalted.

The current Viewing was delayed almost half an hour by reason of the defection of the Meks, and certain hasty improvisations had been necessary. But the gentlefolk of Castle Hagedorn were in no mood to be critical and took no heed of the occasional lapses as a dozen young Peasant bucks struggled to perform unfamiliar tasks. The Phanes were as entracing as ever, bending, twisting, swaying to plangent chords of the lute, fluttering their fingers as if feeling for raindrops, crouching suddenly and gliding, then springing upright as straight as wands, finally bowing and skipping from the platform.

Halfway through the program a Peasant sidled awkwardly into the Rotunda, and mumbled in an urgent manner to the cadet who came to inquire his business. The cadet at once made his way to Hagedorn's polished jet booth. Hagedorn listened, nodded, spoke a few terse words and settled calmly back in his seat as if the message had been of no consequence, and the gentlefolk of the audience were reassured.

The entertainment proceeded. O.Z. Garr's delectable pair made a fine show, but it was generally felt that Lirlin, a young Phane belonging to Isseth Floy Gazuneth, for the first time at a formal showing, made the most captivating display.

The Phanes appeared for a last time, moving all together through a half-improvised minuet, then performing a final half-gay, half-regretful salute, departed the rotunda. For a few moments more the gentlemen and ladies would remain in their booths, sipping essences, discussing the display, arranging affairs and assignations. Hagedorn sat frowning, twisting his hands. Suddenly he rose to his feet. The rotunda instantly became silent.

"I dislike intruding an unhappy note at so pleasant an occasion," said Hagedorn. "But the news has just been given to me, and it is fitting that all should know. Janeil Castle is under attack. The Meks are there in great force, with hundreds of power-wagons. They have circled the castle with a dike which prevents any effective use of the Janeil energy-cannon.

"There is no immediate danger to Janeil, and it is difficult to comprehend what the Meks hope to achieve, the Janeil walls being all of two hundred feet high.

"The news, nevertheless, is somber, and it means that eventually we must expect a similar investment—though it is even more difficult to comprehend how Meks could hope to inconvenience us. Our water derives from four wells sunk deep into the earth. We have great stocks of food. Our energy is derived from the sun. If necessary, we could condense water and synthesize food from the air—at least I have been so assured by our great biochemical theoretician, X.B. Ladisname. Still—this is the news. Make of it what you will. Tomorrow the Council of Notables will meet."

CHAPTER FIVE

1

"Well, then," said Hagedorn to the council, "for once let us dispense with formality. O.Z. Garr: what of our cannon?"

O.Z. Garr, wearing the magnificent gray and green uniform of the Overwhele Dragoons, carefully placed his morion on the table, so that the panache stood erect. "Of twelve cannon, four appear to be functioning correctly. Four have been sabotaged by excision of the power-leads. Four have been sabotaged by some means undetectable to careful investigation. I have commandeered a half-dozen Peasants who demonstrate a modicum of mechanical ability, and have instructed them in detail. They are currently engaged in splicing the leads. This is the extent of my current information in regard to the cannon."

"Moderately good news," said Hagedorn.

"What of the proposed corps of armed Peasants?"

"The project is under way. A.F. Mull and I.A. Berzelius are now inspecting Peasants with a view to recruitment and training. I can make no sanguine projection as to the military effectiveness of such a corps, even if trained and led by such as A.F. Mull, I.A. Berzelius and myself. The Peasants are a mild, ineffectual race, admirably suited to the grubbing of weeds, but with no stomach whatever for fighting."

Hagedorn glanced around the council. "Are there any other suggestions?"

Beaudry spoke in a harsh, angry voice. "Had the villains but left us our power-wagons, we might have mounted the cannon aboard—the Peasants are equal to this, at least. Then we could roll to Janeil and blast the dogs from the rear."

"These Meks seem utter fiends!" declared Aure. "What conceivably do they have in mind? Why, after all these centuries, must they suddenly go mad?"

"We all ask ourselves the same questions," said Hagedorn. "Xanten, you returned from reconnaissance with a captive. Have you attempted to question him?"

"No," said Xanten. "Truth to tell, I haven't thought of him since."

"Why not attempt to question him? Perhaps he can provide a clue or two."

Xanten nodded assent. "I can try. Candidly, I expect to learn nothing."

"Claghorn, you are the Mek expert," said Beaudry. "Would you have thought the creatures capable of so intricate a plot? What do they hope to gain? Our castles?"

"They are certainly capable of precise and meticulous planning," said Claghorn. "Their ruthlessness surprises me—more, possibly, than it should. I have never known them to covet our material possessions, and they show no tendency toward what we consider the concomitants of civilization: fine discriminations of sensation and the like. I have often speculated—I won't dignify the conceit with the status of a theory—that the structural logic of a brain is of rather more consequence than we reckon with. Our own brains are remarkable for their utter lack of rational structure. Considering the haphazard manner in which our thoughts are formed, registered, indexed and recalled, any single rational act becomes a miracle. Perhaps we are incapable of rationality; perhaps all thought is a set of impulses generated by one emotion, monitored by another, ratified by a third. In contrast, the Mek brain is a marvel of what seems to be careful engineering. It is roughly cubical and consists of microscopic cells interconnected by organic fibrils, each a monofilament molecule of negligible electrical resistance. Within each cell is a film of silica, a fluid of variable conductivity and dialectric properties, a cusp of a complex mixture of metallic oxides. The brain is capable of storing great quantities of information in an orderly pattern. No fact is lost, unless it is purposely forgotten, a capacity which the Meks possess. The brain also functions as a radio transceiver, possibly as a radar transmitter and detector, though this again is speculation.

"Where the Mek brain falls short is in its lack of emotional color. One Mek is precisely like another, without any personality differentiation perceptible to us. This, clearly, is a function of their communicative system: unthinkable for a unique personality to develop under these conditions. They served us efficiently and—so we thought—loyally, because they felt nothing about their condition, neither pride in achievement, nor resentment, nor shame. Nothing whatever. They neither loved us nor hated us, nor do they now. It is hard for us to conceive this emotional vacuum, when each of us feels something about everything. We live in a welter of emotions. They are as devoid of emotion as an icecube. They were fed, housed, and maintained in a manner they found satisfactory. Why did they revolt? I have speculated at length, but the single reason which I can formulate seems so grotesque and unreasonable that I refuse to take it seriously. If this after all is the correct explanation . . ." His voice drifted away.

"Well?" demanded O.Z. Garr peremptorily.

"What, then?"

"Then—it is all the same. They are committed to the destruction of the human race. My speculation alters nothing."

Hagedorn turned to Xanten. "All this should assist you in your inquiries."

"I was about to suggest that Claghorn assist me, if he is so inclined," said Xanten.

"As you like," said Claghorn, "though in my opinion the information, no matter what, is irrelevant. Our single concern should be a means to repel them and to save our lives."

"And—except the force of 'panthers' you mentioned at our previous session—you can conceive of no subtle weapon?" asked Hagedorn wistfully. "A device to set up electrical resonances in their brains, or something similar?"

"Not feasible," said Claghorn. "Certain organs in the creatures' brains function as overload switches. Though it is true that during this time they might not be able to communicate." After a moment's reflection he added thoughtfully, "Who knows? A.G. Bernal and Uegus are theoreticians with a profound knowledge of such projections. Perhaps they might construct such a device, or several, against a possible need."

Hagedorn nodded dubiously, and looked toward Uegus. "Is this possible?"

Uegus frowned. " 'Construct'? I can certainly design such an instrument. But the components —where? Scattered through the storerooms helter-skelter, some functioning, others not. To achieve anything meaningful I must become no better than an apprentice, a Mek." He became incensed, and his voice hardened. "I find it hard to believe that I should be forced to point out this fact. Do you hold me and my talents then of such small worth?"

Hagedorn hastened to reassure him. "Of course not! I for one would never think of impugning your dignity."

"Never!" agreed Claghorn. "Nevertheless, during this present emergency, we will find indignities imposed upon us by events, unless now we impose them upon ourselves."

"Very well," said Uegus, a humorless smile trembling at his lips. "You shall come with me to the storeroom. I will point out the components to be brought forth and assembled, you shall perform the toil. What do you say to that?"

"I say yes, gladly, if it will be of real utility. However, I can hardly perform the labor for a dozen different theoreticians. Will any others serve beside myself?"

No one responded. Silence was absolute, as if every gentleman present held his breath.

Hagedorn started to speak, but Claghorn interrupted. "Pardon, Hagedorn, but here, finally we are stuck upon a basic principle, and it must be settled now."

Hagedorn looked desperately around the council. "Has anyone relevant comment?"

"Claghorn must do as his innate nature compels," declared O.Z. Garr in the silkiest of voices. "I cannot dictate to him. As for myself, I can never demean my status as a gentleman of Hagedorn. This creed is as natural to me as drawing breath; if ever it is compromised I become a travesty of a gentleman, a grotesque mask of myself. This is Castle Hagedorn, and we represent the culmination of human civilization. Any compromise therefore becomes degradation; any expedient diminution of our standards becomes dishonor. I have heard the word 'emergency' used. What a deplorable sentiment! To dignify the rat-like snappings and gnashings of such as the Meks with the word 'emergency' is to my mind unworthy of a gentleman of Hagedorn!"

A murmur of approval went around the council table.

Claghorn leaned far back in his seat, chin on his chest, as if in relaxation. His clear blue eyes went from face to face, then returned to O.Z. Garr whom he studied with dispassionate interest. "Obviously you direct your words to me," he said, "and I appreciate their malice. But this is a small matter." He looked away from O.Z. Garr, to stare up at the massive diamond and emerald chandelier. "More important is the fact that the council as a whole, in spite of my earnest persuasion, seems to endorse your viewpoint. I can urge, expostulate, insinuate no longer, and I will now leave Castle Hagedorn. I find the atmosphere stifling. I trust that you survive the attack of the Meks, though I doubt that you will. They are a clever, resourceful race, untroubled by qualms or preconceptions, and we have long underestimated their quality."

Claghorn rose from his seat, inserted the ivory tablet into its socket. "I bid you all farewell."

Hagedorn hastily jumped to his feet and held forth his arms imploringly. "Do not depart in anger, Claghorn! Reconsider! We need your wisdom, your expertise!"

"Assuredly you do," said Claghorn. "But even more, you need to act upon the advice I have already extended. Until then, we have no common ground, and any further interchange is futile and tiresome." He made a brief, all-inclusive salute and departed the chamber.

Hagedorn slowly resumed his seat. The others made uneasy motions, coughed, looked up at the chandelier, studied their ivory tablets. O.Z. Garr muttered something to B.F. Wyas who sat beside him, and nodded solemnly. Hagedorn spoke in a subdued voice: "We will miss the presence of Claghorn, his penetrating if unorthodox insights . . . We have accomplished little. Uegus, perhaps you will give thought to the projector under discussion. Xanten, you were to question the captive Mek. O.Z. Garr, you undoubtedly will see to the repair of the energy cannon. . . . Aside from these small matters, it appears that we have evolved no general plan of action, to help either ourselves or Janeil.

Marune spoke. "What of the other castles? Are they still extant? We have had no news. I suggest that we send Birds to each castle, to learn their condition."

Hagedorn nodded. "Yes, this is a wise motion. Perhaps you will see to this, Marune?"

"I will do so."

"Good. We will now adjourn."

2

The Birds dispatched by Marune of Aure, one by one returned. Their reports were similar:

"Sea Island is deserted. Marble columns are tumbled along the beach. Pearl Dome is collapsed. Corpses float in the Water Garden."

"Maraval reeks of death. Gentlemen, Peasants, Phane—all dead. Alas! Even the Birds have departed!"

"Delora: *a ros ros ros!* A dismal scene! No sign of life!"

"Alume is desolate. The great wooden door is smashed. The Green Flame is extinguished."

"There is nothing at Halcyon. The Peasants were driven into a pit."

"Tuang: silence."

"Morninglight: death."

CHAPTER SIX

1

Three days later, Xanten constrained six Birds to a lift chair, directed them first on a wide sweep around the castle, then south to Far Valley.

The Birds aired their usual complaints, then bounded down the deck in great ungainly hops which threatened to throw Xanten immediately to the pavement. At last gaining the air, they flew up in a spiral; Castle Hagedorn became an intricate miniature far below, each House marked by its unique cluster of turrets and eyries, its own eccentric roof line, its long streaming pennon.

The Birds performed the prescribed circle, skimming the crags and pines of North Ridge; then, setting wings aslant the upstream, they coasted away toward Far Valley.

Over the pleasant Hagedorn domain flew the Birds and Xanten: over orchards, fields, vineyards, Peasant villages. They crossed Lake Maude with its pavilions and docks, the meadows beyond where the Hagedorn cattle and sheep grazed, and presently came to Far Valley, at the limit of Hagedorn lands.

Xanten indicated where he wished to alight; the Birds, who would have preferred a site closer to the village where they could have watched all that transpired, grumbled and cried out in wrath and set Xanten down so roughly that had he not been alert the shock would have pitched him head over heels.

Xanten alighted without elegance but at least remained on his feet. "Await me here!" he ordered. "Do not stray; attempt no flamboyant tricks among the liftstraps. When I return I wish to see six quiet Birds, in neat formation, lift-straps untwisted and untangled. No bickering, mind you! No loud caterwauling, to attract unfavorable comment! Let all be as I have ordered!"

The Birds sulked, stamped their feet, ducked aside their necks, made insulting comments just under the level of Xanten's hearing. Xanten, turning them a final glare of admonition, walked down the lane which led to the village.

The vines were heavy with ripe blackberries and a number of the girls of the village filled baskets. Among them was the girl O.Z. Garr had thought to preempt for his personal use. As Xanten passed, he halted and performed a courteous salute. "We have met before, if my recollection is correct."

The girl smiled, a half-rueful, half-whimsical smile. "Your recollection serves you well. We met at Hagedorn, where I was taken a captive. And later, when you conveyed me here, after dark, though I could not see your face." She extended her basket. "Are you hungry? Will you eat?"

Xanten took several berries. In the course of the conversation he learned that the girl's name was Glys Meadowsweet, that her parents were not known to her, but were presumably gentlefolk of Castle Hagedorn who had exceeded their birth tally. Xanten examined her even more carefully than before but could see resemblance to none of the Hagedorn families. "You might derive from Castle Delora. If there is any family resemblance I can detect, it is to the Cosanzas of Delora—a family noted for the beauty of its ladies."

"You are not married?" she asked artlessly.

"No," said Xanten, and indeed he had dissolved his relationship with Araminta only the day before. "What of you?"

She shook her head. "I would never be gathering blackberries otherwise; it is work reserved for maidens. . . . Why do you come to Far Valley?"

"For two reasons. The first to see you." Xanten heard himself say this with surprise. But it was true, he realized with another small shock of surprise. "I have never spoken with you properly and I have always wondered if you were as charming and gay as you are beautiful."

The girl shrugged and Xanten could not be sure whether she were pleased or not, compliments from gentlemen sometimes setting the stage for a sorry aftermath. "Well, no matter, I came also to speak to Claghorn."

"He is yonder," she said in a voice toneless, even cool, and pointed. "He occupies that cottage." She returned to her blackberry picking. Xanten bowed and proceeded to the cottage the girl had indicated.

Claghorn, wearing loose knee-length breeches of gray homespun, worked with an axe chopping faggots into stove-lengths. At the sight of Xanten he halted his toil, leaned on the axe and mopped his forehead. "Ah, Xanten. I am pleased to see you. How are the folk of Castle Hagedorn?"

"As before. There is little to report, even had I come to bring you news."

"Indeed, indeed?" Claghorn leaned on the axe handle, surveying Xanten with a bright blue gaze.

"At our last meeting," went on Xanten, "I agreed to question the captive Mek. After doing so I am distressed that you were not at hand to assist, so that you might have resolved certain ambiguities in the responses."

"Speak on," said Claghorn. "Perhaps I shall be able to do so now."

"After the council meeting I descended immediately to the storeroom where the Mek was confined. It lacked nutriment; I gave it syrup and a pail of water, which it sipped sparingly, then evinced a desire for minced clams. I summoned kitchen help and sent them for this commodity and the Mek ingested several pints. As I have indicated, it was an unusual Mek, standing as tall as myself and lacking a syrup sac. I conveyed it to a different chamber, a storeroom for brown plush furniture, and ordered it to a seat.

"I looked at the Mek and it looked at me. The quills which I removed were growing back; probably it could at least receive from Meks elsewhere. It seemed a superior beast, showing neither obsequiousness nor respect, and answered my questions without hesitation.

"First I remarked: 'The gentlefolk of the castles are astounded by the revolt of the Meks. We had assumed that your life was satisfactory. Were we wrong?'

" 'Evidently.' I am sure that this was the word signaled, though never had I suspected the Meks of dryness or wit of any sort.

" 'Very well then,' I said. 'In what manner?'

" 'Surely it is obvious,' he said. 'We no longer wished to toil at your behest. We wished to conduct our lives by our own traditional standards.'

"The response surprised me. I was unaware

that the Meks possessed standards of any kind, much less traditional standards."

Claghorn nodded. "I have been similarly surprised by the scope of the Mek mentality."

"I reproached the Mek: 'Why kill? Why destroy our lives in order to augment your own?' As soon as I had put the question I realized that it had been unhappily phrased. The Mek, I believe, realized the same; however, in reply he signaled something very rapidly which I believe was: 'We knew we must act with decisiveness. Your own protocol made this necessary. We might have returned to Etamin Nine, but we prefer this world Earth, and will make it our own, with our own great slipways, tubs and basking ramps.'

"This seemed clear enough, but I sensed an adumbration extending yet beyond. I said, "Comprehensible. But why kill, why destroy? You might have taken yourself to a different region. We could not have molested you.'

" 'Infeasible, by your own thinking. A world is too small for two competing races. You intended to send us back to dismal Etamin Nine.'

" 'Ridiculous!' I said. 'Fantasy, absurdity. Do you take me for a mooncalf?'

" 'No,' the creature insisted. 'Two of Castle Hagedorn's notables were seeking the highest post. One assured us that, if elected, this would become his life's aim.'

" 'A grotesque misunderstanding,' I told him.

'One man, a lunatic, can not speak for all men!'

" 'No? One Mek speaks for all Meks. We think with one mind. Are not men of a like sort?"

" 'Each thinks for himself. The lunatic who assured you of this tomfoolery is an evil man. But at least matters are clear. We do not propose to send you to Etamin Nine. Will you withdraw from Janeil, take yourselves to a far land and leave us in peace?'

" 'No,' he said. 'Affairs have proceeded too far. We will now destroy all men. The truth of the statement is clear: one world is too small for two races.'

" 'Unluckily, then, I must kill you,' I told him. 'Such acts are not to my liking, but, with opportunity, you would kill as many gentlemen as possible.' At this the creature sprang upon me, and I killed it with an easier mind than had it sat staring.

"Now, you know all. It seems that either you or O.Z. Garr stimulated the cataclysm. O.Z. Garr? Unlikely. Impossible. Hence, you, Claghorn, you! have this weight upon your soul!"

Claghorn frowned down at the axe. "Weight, yes. Guilt, no. Ingenuousness, yes; wickedness, no."

Xanten stood back. "Claghorn, your coolness astounds me! Before, when rancorous folk like O.Z. Garr conceived you a lunatic—"

"Peace, Xanten!" exclaimed Claghorn. "This extravagant breast-beating becomes maladroit. What have I done wrong? My fault is that I tried too much. Failure is tragic, but a phthisic face hanging over the cup of the future is worse. I meant to become Hagedorn, I would have sent the slaves home. I failed, the slaves revolted. So do not speak another word. I am bored with the subject. You can not imagine how your bulging eyes and your concave spine oppress me."

"Bored you may be," cried Xanten. "You decry my eyes, my spine—but what of the thousands dead?"

"How long would they live in any event? Lives as cheap as fish in the sea. I suggest that you put by your reproaches and devote a similar energy to saving yourself. Do you realize that a means exists? You stare at me blankly. I assure you that what I say is true, but you will never learn the means from me."

"Claghorn," said Xanten, "I flew to this spot intending to blow your arrogant head from your body—" Claghorn, no longer heeding, had returned to his wood-chopping.

"Claghorn!" cried Xanten. "Attend me!"

"Xanten, take your outcries elsewhere, if you please. Remonstrate with your Birds."

Xanten swung on his heel and marched back down the lane. The girls picking berries looked at him questioningly and moved aside. Xanten halted to look up and down the lane. Glys

Meadowsweet was nowhere to be seen. In a few fury he continued. He stopped short. On a fallen tree a hundred feet from the Birds sat Glys Meadowsweet, examining a blade of grass as if it had been an astonishing artifact of the past. The Birds, for a marvel, had actually obeyed him and waited in a fair semblance of order.

Xanten looked up toward the heavens, kicked at the turf. He drew a deep breath and approached to Glys Meadowsweet. He noted that she had tucked a flower into her long loose hair.

After a second or two she looked up and searched his face. "Why are you so angry?"

Xanten slapped his thigh, then seated himself beside her. " 'Angry'? No. I am out of my mind with frustration. Claghorn is as obstreperous as a sharp rock. He knows how Castle Hagedorn can be saved but he will not divulge his secret."

Glys Meadowsweet laughed—an easy, merry sound, like nothing Xanten had ever heard at Castle Hagedorn. "Secret? When even I know it?"

"It must be a secret," said Xanten. "He will not tell me."

"Listen. If you fear the Birds will hear, I will whisper." She spoke a few words into his ear.

Perhaps the sweet breath befuddled Xanten's mind. But the explicit essence of the revelation failed to strike home into his consciousness. He made a sound of sour amusement. "No secret there. Only what the prehistoric Scythians termed *bathos*. Dishonor to the gentlemen! Do we dance with the Peasants? Do we serve the Birds essences and discuss with them the sheen of our Phanes?"

" 'Dishonor,' then?" She jumped to her feet. "Then it is also dishonor for you to talk to me, to sit here with me, to make ridiculous suggestions—"

"I made no suggestions!" protested Xanten. "I sit here in all decorum—"

"Too much decorum, too much honor!" With a display of passion which astounded Xanten, Glys Meadowsweet tore the flower from her hair and hurled it at the ground. "There. Hence!"

"No," said Xanten in sudden humility. He bent, picked up the flower, kissed it, replaced it in her hair. "I am not over-honorable. I will try my best." He put his arms on her shoulders, but she held him away.

"Tell me," she inquired with a very mature severity, "do you own any of those peculiar insect-women?"

"I? Phanes? I own no Phanes."

With this Glys Meadowsweet relaxed and allowed Xanten to embrace her, while the Birds clucked, guffawed and made vulgar scratching sounds with their wings.

CHAPTER SEVEN

1

The summer waned. On June 30 Janeil and Hagedorn celebrated the Fete of Flowers, even though the dike was rising high around Janeil. Shortly after, Xanten flew six select Birds into Castle Janeil by night, and proposed to the council that the population be evacuated by Bird-lift—as many as possible, as many who wished to leave. The council listened with stony faces and without comment passed on to a consideration of other affairs.

Xanten returned to Castle Hagedorn. Using the most careful methods, speaking only to trusted comrades, Xanten enlisted thirty or forty cadets and gentlemen to his persuasion, though inevitably he could not keep the doctrinal thesis of his program secret.

The first reaction of the traditionalists was mockery and charges of poltroonery. At

Xanten's insistence, challenges were neither issued nor accepted by his hotblooded associates.

On the evening of September 9 Castle Janeil fell. The news was brought to Castle Hagedorn by excited Birds who told the grim tale again and again in voices ever more hysterical.

Hagedorn, now gaunt and weary, automatically called a council meeting; it took note of the gloomy circumstances. "We, then, are the last castle! The Meks cannot conceivably do us harm; they can build dikes around our castle walls for twenty years and only work themselves to distraction. We are secure; but yet it is a strange and portentous thought to realize that at last, here at Castle Hagedorn, live the last gentlemen of the race!"

Xanten spoke in a voice strained with earnest conviction: "Twenty years—fifty years—what difference to the Meks? Once they surround us, once they deploy, we are trapped. Do you comprehend that now is our last opportunity to escape the great cage that Castle Hagedorn is to become?"

" 'Escape,' Xanten? What a word! For shame!" hooted O.Z. Garr. "Take your wretched band, escape! To steppe or swamp or tundra! Go as you like, with your poltroons, but be good enough to give over these incessant alarms!"

"Garr, I have found conviction since I become

a 'poltroon.' Survival is good morality. I have this from the mouth of a noted savant."

"Bah! Such as whom?"

"A.G. Philidor, if you must be informed of every detail."

O.Z. Garr clapped his hand to his forehead. "Do you refer to Philidor, the Expiationist? He is of the most extreme stripe, an Expiationist to out-expiate all the rest! Xanten, be sensible, if you please!"

"There are years ahead for all of us," said Xanten in a wooden voice, "if we free ourselves from the castle."

"But the castle is our life!" declared Hagedorn. "In essence, Xanten, what would we be without the castle? Wild animals? Nomads?"

"We would be alive."

O.Z. Garr gave a snort of disgust and turned away to inspect a wall-hanging.

Hagedorn shook his head in doubt and perplexity. Beaudry threw his hands up into the air. "Xanten, you have the effect of unnerving us all. You come in here and inflict this dreadful sense of urgency—but why? In Castle Hagedorn we are as safe as in our mothers' arms. What do we gain by throwing aside all—honor, dignity, comfort, civilized niceties—for no other reason than to slink through the wilderness?"

"Janeil was safe," said Xanten. "Today where is Janeil? Death, mildewed cloth, sour wine. What we gain by *slinking* is the assurance of survival. And I plan much more than simple *slinking*."

"I can conceive of a hundred occasions when death is better than life!" snapped Isseth. "Must I die in dishonor and disgrace? Why may my last years not be passed in dignity?"

Into the room came B.F. Robarth. "Councilmen, the Meks approach Castle Hagedorn."

Hagedorn cast a wild look around the chamber. "Is there a consensus? What must we do?"

Xanten threw up his hands. "Everyone must do as he thinks best! I argue no more: I am done. Hagedorn, will you adjourn the council so that we may be about our affairs? I to my *slinking?*"

"Council is adjourned," said Hagedorn, and all went to stand on the ramparts.

Up the avenue into the castle trooped Peasants from the surrounding countryside, packets slung over their shoulders. Across the valley, at the edge of Bartholomew Forest, was a clot of power-wagons and an amorphous brown-gold mass: Meks.

Aure pointed west. "Look—there they come, up the Long Swale." He turned, peered east. "And look, there at Bambridge: Meks!"

By common consent, all swung about to scan North Ridge. O.Z. Garr pointed to a quiet line of brown-gold shapes. "There they wait, the vermin! They have penned us in! Well, then, let them wait!" He swung away, rode the lift down to the plaza, and crossed swiftly to Zumbeld House, where he worked the rest of the afternoon with his Gloriana, of whom he expected great things.

2

The following day the Meks formalized the investment. Around Castle Hagedorn a great circle of Mek activity made itself apparent: sheds, warehouses, barracks. Within this periphery, just beyond the range of the energy cannon, power-wagons thrust up mounds of dirt.

During the night these mounds lengthened toward the castle, similarly the night after. At last the purpose of the mounds became clear: they were a protective cover above passages or tunnels leading toward the crag on which Castle Hagedorn rested.

The following day several of the mounds reached the base of the crag. Presently a succession of power-wagons loaded with rubble began to flow from the far end. They issued, dumped their loads, and once again entered the tunnels.

Eight of these above-ground tunnels had been established. From each trundled endless loads of dirt and rock, gnawed from the crag on which Castle Hagedorn sat. To the gentlefolk who crowded the parapets the meaning of the work at last became clear.

"They make no attempt to bury us," said Hagedorn. "They merely mine out the crag from below us!"

On the sixth day of the siege, a great segment of the hillside shuddered, slumped, and a tall pinnacle of rock reaching almost up to the base of the walls collapsed.

"If this continues," muttered Beaudry, "our time will be less than that of Janeil."

"Come then," called O.Z. Garr, suddenly active. "Let us try our energy cannon. We'll blast open their wretched tunnels, and then what will the rascals do?" He went to the nearest emplacement and shouted down for Peasants to remove the tarpaulin.

Xanten, who happened to be standing nearby, said, "Allow me to assist you." He jerked away the tarpaulin. "Shoot now, if you will."

O.Z. Garr stared at him uncomprehendingly, then leaped forward and swiveled the great projector about so that it aimed at a mound. He pulled the switch; the air crackled in front of the ringed snout, rippled, flickered with purple sparks. The target area steamed, became black, then dark red, then slumped into an incandescent crater. But the underlying earth, twenty feet in thickness, afforded too much insulation; the molten puddle became white-hot but failed to spread or deepen. The energy cannon gave a sudden chatter, as electricity short-circuited through corroded insulation. The cannon went dead. O.Z. Garr inspected the mechanism in anger and disappointment; then, with a gesture of repugnance, he turned away. The cannons were clearly of limited effectiveness.

Two hours later, on the east side of the crag, another great sheet of rock collapsed, and just before sunset a similar mass sheared from the western face, where the wall of the castle rose almost in an uninterrupted line from the cliff below.

At midnight Xanten and those of his persuasion, with their children and consorts, departed Castle Hagedorn. Six teams of Birds shuttled from the flight deck to a meadow near Far Valley, and long before dawn had transported the entire group. There were none to bid them farewell.

3

A week later another section of the east cliff fell away, taking a length of rock-melt buttress with it. At the tunnel mouths the piles of excavated rubble had become alarmingly large.

The terraced south face of the crag was the least disturbed, the most spectacular damage having occurred to east and west. Suddenly, a month after the initial assault, a great section of the terrace slumped forward, leaving an irregular crevasse which interrupted the avenue and hurled down the statues of former notables emplaced at intervals along the avenue's balustrade.

Hagedorn called a council meeting. "Circumstances," he said in a wan attempt at facetiousness, "have not bettered themselves. Our most pessimistic expectations have been exceeded: a dismal situation. I confess that I do not relish the prospect of toppling to my death among all my smashed belongings."

Aure made a desperate gesture. "A similar thought haunts me! Death—what of that? All must die! But when I think of my precious belongings I become sick. My books trampled! my fragile vases smashed! my tabards ripped! my rugs buried! my Phanes strangled! my heirloom chandeliers flung aside! These are my nightmares."

"Your possessions are no less precious than any others," said Beaudry shortly. "Still, they have no life of their own; when we are gone, who cares what happens to them?"

Marune winced. "A year ago I put down eighteen dozen flasks of prime essence; twelve dozen Green Rain; three each of Balthazar and Faidor. Think of these, if you would contemplate tragedy!"

"Had we only known!" groaned Aure. "I

would have—I would have . . ." His voice trailed away.

O.Z. Garr stamped his foot in impatience. "Let us avoid lamentation at all costs! We had a choice, remember? Xanten beseeched us to flee; now he and his like go skulking and foraging through the north mountains with the Expiationists. We chose to remain, for better or worse, and unluckily the worse is occurring. We must accept the fact like gentlemen."

To this the council gave melancholy assent. Hagedorn brought forth a flask of priceless Rhadamanth, and poured with a prodigality which previously would have been unthinkable. "Since we have no future—to our glorious past!"

That night disturbances were noted here and there around the ring of Mek investment: flames at four separate points, a faint sound of hoarse shouting. On the following day it seemed that the tempo of activity had lessened a trifle.

During the afternoon, however, a vast segment of the east cliff fell away. A moment later, as if after majestic deliberation, the tall east wall split off and toppled, leaving the backs of six great houses exposed to the open sky.

An hour after sunset a team of Birds settled to the flight-deck. Xanten jumped from the seat. He ran down the circular staircase to the ramparts and came down to the plaza by Hagedorn's palace.

Hagedorn, summoned by a kinsman, came forth to stare at Xanten in surprise. "What do you do here? We expected you to be safely north with the Expiationists!"

"The Expiationists are not safely north," said Xanten. "They have joined the rest of us. We are fighting."

Hagedorn's jaw dropped. "Fighting? The gentlemen are fighting Meks?"

"As vigorously as possible."

Hagedorn shook his head in wonder. "The Expiationists too? I understood that they had planned to flee north."

"Some have done so, including A.G. Philidor. There are factions among the Expiationists just as here. Most are not ten miles distant. The same with the Nomads. Some have taken their power-wagons and fled. The rest kill Meks with fanatic fervor. Last night you saw our work. We fire four storage warehouses, destroyed syrup tanks, killed a hundred or more Meks, as well as a dozen power-wagons. We suffered losses, which hurt us because there are few of us and many Meks. This is why I am here. We need more men. Come fight beside us!"

Hagedorn turned, motioning to the great central plaza. "I will call forth the folk from their Houses. Talk to everyone."

4

The Birds, complaining bitterly at the unprecedented toil, worked all night, transporting the gentlemen who, sobered by the imminent destruction of Castle Hagedorn, were now willing to abandon all scruples and fight for their lives. The staunch traditionalists still refused to compromise their honor, but Xanten gave them cheerful assurance: "Remain here, then, prowling the castle like so many furtive rats. Take what comfort you can in the fact that you are being protected; the future holds little else for you."

And many who heard him stalked away in disgust.

Xanten turned to Hagedorn. "What of you? Do you come or do you stay?"

Hagedorn heaved a deep sigh, almost a groan. "Castle Hagedorn is at an end. No matter what the eventuality. I come with you."

5

The situation had suddenly altered. The Meks, established in a loose ring around Castle Hagedorn, had calculated upon no resistance from the countryside and little from the castle.

They had established their barracks and syrup depots with thought only for convenience and none for defense; raiding parties, consequently, were able to approach, inflict damages and withdraw before sustaining serious losses of their own. Those Meks posted along North Ridge were harassed almost continuously, and finally were driven down with many losses. The circle around Castle Hagedorn became a cusp; then two days later, after the destruction of five more syrup depots, the Meks drew back even farther. Throwing up earthworks before the two tunnels leading under the south face of the crag, they established a more or less tenable defensive position, but now instead of beleaguering, they became the beleaguered, even though power-wagons of broken rock still issued from the crag.

Within the area thus defended the Meks concentrated their remaining syrup stocks, tools, weapons, ammunition. The area outside the earthworks was floodlit after dark and guarded by Meks armed with pellet guns, making any frontal assault impractical.

For a day the raiders kept to the shelter of the surrounding orchards, appraising the new situation. Then a new tactic was attempted. Six light carriages were improvised and loaded with bladders of a light inflammable oil, with a fire grenade attached. To each of these carriages ten Birds were harnessed, and at midnight sent aloft, with a man for each carriage. Flying high, the

Birds then glided down through the darkness over the Mek position, where the fire bombs were dropped. The area instantly seethed with flame. The syrup depot burned; the power-wagons, awakened by the flames, rolled frantically back and forth, crushing Meks and stores, colliding with each other, adding vastly to the terror of the fire. The Meks who survived took shelter in the tunnels. Certain of the floodlights were extinguished and taking advantage of the confusion, the men attacked the earthworks. After a short, bitter battle, the men killed all the sentinels and took up positions commanding the mouths of the tunnels, which now contained all that remained of the Mek army. It seemed as if the Mek uprising had been put down.

CHAPTER EIGHT

1

The flames died. The human warriors—three hundred men from the castle, two hundred Expiationists and about three hundred Nomads—gathered about the tunnel mouth and, during the balance of the night, considered methods to deal with the immured Meks. At sunrise, those men of Castle Hagedorn whose children and consorts were yet inside went to bring them forth. With them, upon their return, came a group of castle gentlemen: among them Beaudry, O.Z. Garr, Isseth, and Aure. They greeted their one-time peers, Hagedorn, Xanten, Claghorn and others, crisply, but with a certain austere detachment which recognized that the loss of prestige incurred by those who fought Meks as if they were equals.

"Now what is to happen?" Beaudry inquired of Hagedorn. "The Meks are trapped but you can't bring them forth. Not impossibly they have syrup stored within for the power-wagons; they may well survive for months."

O.Z. Garr, assessing the situation from the standpoint of a military theoretician, came forward with a plan of action. "Fetch down the cannon—or have your underlings do so—and mount them on power-wagons. When the vermin are sufficiently weak, roll the cannon in and wipe out all but a labor force for the castle: we formerly worked four hundred, and this should suffice."

"Ha!" exclaimed Xanten. "It gives me great pleasure to inform you that this will never be. If any Meks survive they will repair the spaceships and instruct us in the maintenance and we will then transport them and Peasants back to their native worlds."

"How then do you expect us to maintain our lives?" demanded Garr coldly.

"You have the syrup generator. Fit yourself with sacs and drink syrup."

Garr tilted back his head, stared coldly down his nose. "This is your voice, yours alone, and your insolent opinion. Others are to be heard from. Hagedorn—you were once a gentleman. Is this also your philosophy, that civilization should wither?"

"It need not wither," said Hagedorn, "provided that all of us—you as well as we—toil for it. There can be no more slaves. I have become convinced of this."

O.Z. Garr turned on his heel, swept back up the avenue into the castle, followed by the most traditional-minded of his comrades. A few moved aside and talked among themselves in low tones, with one or two black looks for Xanten and Hagedorn.

From the ramparts of the castle came a sudden outcry: "The Meks! They are taking the castle! They swarm up the lower passages! Attack, save us!"

The men below stared up in consternation. Even as they looked, the castle portals swung shut.

"How is this possible?" demanded Hagedorn. "I swear all entered the tunnels!"

"It is only too clear," said Xanten bitterly. "While they undermined, they drove a tunnel up to the lower levels!"

Hagedorn started forward as if he would charge up the crag alone, then halted. "We must drive them out. Unthinkable that they pillage our castle!"

"Unfortunately," said Claghorn, "the walls bar us as effectively as they did the Meks."

"We can send up a force by Bird-car! Once we consolidate, we can hunt them down, exterminate them."

Claghorn shook his head. "They can wait on the ramparts and flight-deck and shoot down the Birds as they approach. Even if we secured a foothold there would be great bloodshed: one of us killed for every one of them. And they still outnumber us three or four to one."

Hagedorn groaned. "The thought of them reveling among my possessions, strutting about in my clothes, swilling my essences—it sickens me!"

"Listen!" said Claghorn. From on high they heard the horse yells of men, the crackle of energy-cannon. "Some of them, at least, hold out on ramparts!"

Xanten went to a nearby group of Birds who were for once awed and subdued by events. "Lift me up above the castle, out of range of the pellets, but where I can see what the Meks do!"

"Care, take care!" croaked one of the Birds. "Ill things occur at the castle."

"Never mind; convey me up, above the ramparts!"

The Birds lifted him, swung in a great circle around the crag and above the castle, sufficiently distant to be safe from the Mek pellet-guns. Beside those cannon which yet operated stood thirty men and women. Between the great Houses, the Rotunda and the Palace, everywhere the cannon could not be brought to bear, swarmed Meks. The plaza was littered with corpses: gentlemen, ladies and their children—all those who had elected to remain at Castle Hagedorn.

At one of the cannon stood O.Z. Garr. Spying

Xanten he gave a shout of hysterical rage, swung up the cannon, fired a bolt. The Birds, screaming, tried to swerve aside, but the bolt smashed two. Birds, car, Xanten, fell in a great tangle. By some miracle, the four yet alive caught their balance and a hundred feet from the ground, with a frenzied groaning effort, they slowed their fall, steadied, hovered an instant, sank to the ground. Xanten staggered free of the tangle. Men came running. "Are you safe?" called Claghorn.

"Safe, yes. Frightened as well." Xanten took a deep breath, and went to sit on an outcrop of rock.

"What's happening up there?" asked Claghorn.

"All dead," said Xanten, "all but a score. Garr has gone mad. He fired on me."

"Look! Meks on the ramparts!" cried A.L. Morgan.

"There!" cried someone else. "Men! They jump! . . . No, they are flung."

Some were men, some were Meks whom they had dragged with them; with awful slowness they toppled to their deaths. No more fell. Castle Hagedorn was in the hands of the Meks.

Xanten considered the complex silhouette, at once so familiar and so strange. "They can't hope to hold out. We need only destroy the suncells, and they can synthesize no syrup."

"Let us do it now," said Claghorn, "before they think of this and man the cannon. Birds!"

He went off to give the orders, and forty Birds, each clutching two rocks the size of a man's head, flapped up, circled the castle and presently returned to report the sun-cells destroyed.

Xanten said, "All that remains is to seal the tunnel entrances against a sudden eruption, which might catch us off guard—then patience."

"What of the Peasants in the stables—and the Phanes?" asked Hagedorn in a forlorn voice.

Xanten gave his head a slow shake. "He who was not an Expiationist before must become one now."

Claghorn muttered, "They can survive two months—no more."

But two months passed, and three months, and four months: then one morning the great portals opened and a haggard Mek stumbled forth. He signaled: "Men: we starve. We have maintained your treasures. Give us our lives or we destroy all before we die."

Claghorn responded: "These are our terms. We give you your lives. You must clean the castle, remove and bury the corpses. You must repair the spaceships and teach us all you know regarding them. We will then transport you to Etamin Nine."

2

Five years later Xanten and Glys Meadowsweet, with their two children, had reason to travel north from their home near Sande River. They took occasion to visit Castle Hagedorn, where now lived only two or three dozen folk, among them Hagedorn.

He had aged, so it seemed to Xanten. His hair was white; his face, once bluff and hearty, had become thin, almost waxen. Xanten could not determine his mood.

They stood in the shade of a walnut tree, with castle and crag looming above them. "This is now a great museum," said Hagedorn. "I am curator, and this will be the function of all the Hagedorns who come after me, for there is incalculable treasure to guard and maintain. Already the feeling of antiquity has come to the castle. The Houses are alive with ghosts. I see them often, especially on the nights of the fetes. . . . Ah, those were the times, were they not, Xanten?"

"Yes, indeed," said Xanten. He touched the heads of his two children. "Still, I have no wish to return to them. We are men now, on our own world, as we never were before."

Hagedorn gave a somewhat regretful assent. He looked up at the vast structure, as if now were the first occasion he had laid eyes on it.

"The folk of the future—what will they think of Castle Hagedorn? Its treasures, its books, its tabards?"

"They will come, they will marvel," said Xanten. "Almost as I do today."

"There is much at which to marvel. Will you come within, Xanten? There are still flasks of noble essence laid by."

"Thank you, no," said Xanten. "There is too much to stir old memories. We will go our way, and I think immediately."

Hagedorn nodded sadly. "I understand very well. I myself am often given to reverie these days. Well then, goodbye, and journey home with pleasure."

"We will do so, Hagedorn. Thank you and good-bye."

About the Author. . . .

Jack Vance was born in 1920, served in the U.S. Merchant Marine during World War II, and has supported himself at times by jobs ranging from construction worker to jazz musician. He has written more than forty novels and seventy-five shorter works in fantasy, mystery, horror, and science fiction. He was one of the primary writers for the popular "Captain Video" TV series. Some of his awards include the Hugo (for THE DRAGON MASTERS and THE LAST CASTLE), the Nebula (for THE LAST CASTLE), and the Mystery Writers of America Edgar Award (for THE MAN IN THE CAGE). Vance is known for a sly wit, a magnificently colorful imagination, and characters who combine the heroic and the absurd in quantities that approximate the human condition more accurately than most writers ever dream of. He is a fine sailor, plays a mean banjo, and lives in Oakland, California with his family.

WHY WASTE YOUR PRECIOUS PENNIES ON GAS OR YOUR VALUABLE TIME ON LINE AT THE BOOKSTORE?

We will send you, FREE, our 28 page catalogue, filled with a wide range of Ace Science Fiction paperback titles—we've got something for every reader's pleasure.

Here's your chance to add to your personal library, with all the convenience of shopping by mail. There's no need to be without a book to enjoy—request your *free* catalogue today.

CONAN

ALL TWELVE TITLES AVAILABLE FROM ACE
$2.25 EACH

☐ 11630 **CONAN, #1**

☐ 11631 **CONAN OF CIMMERIA, #2**

☐ 11632 **CONAN THE FREEBOOTER, #3**

☐ 11633 **CONAN THE WANDERER, #4**

☐ 11634 **CONAN THE ADVENTURER, #5**

☐ 11635 **CONAN THE BUCCANEER, #6**

☐ 11636 **CONAN THE WARRIOR, #7**

☐ 11637 **CONAN THE USURPER, #8**

☐ 11638 **CONAN THE CONQUEROR, #9**

☐ 11639 **CONAN THE AVENGER, #10**

☐ 11640 **CONAN OF AQUILONIA, #11**

☐ 11641 **CONAN OF THE ISLES, #12**

Available wherever paperbacks are sold or use this coupon.

ANDRE NORTON

WITCH WORLD SERIES

☐ 89705   **WITCH WORLD** $1.95

☐ 87875   **WEB OF THE WITCH WORLD** $1.95

☐ 80806   **THREE AGAINST THE WITCH WORLD** $1.95

☐ 87323   **WARLOCK OF THE WITCH WORLD** $2.25

☐ 77556   **SORCERESS OF THE WITCH WORLD** $2.50

☐ 94255   **YEAR OF THE UNICORN** $2.50

☐ 82349   **TREY OF SWORDS** $2.25

☐ 95491   **ZARSTHOR'S BANE** (Illustrated) $2.50
